THE ITA~~LIAN~~

The Dallori brother~~s~~

Suave and sophisti~~cated,~~
Antonio and Marco are 100% Italian.

Antonio is cool-headed and in control,
but he's definitely hot-blooded.
And single mum Laura Bright is testing his resolve…
Will Antonio be able to use his irresistible
Latin looks to tempt Laura down the aisle…?

Marco's determined to be a bachelor;
no woman is going to catch him! But when he catches
the bouquet at Antonio's wedding he starts to wonder
if soon he'll be the one saying 'I do'!

Look out for Marco's story
coming soon in Medical Romance™!

Recent titles by the same author:

THE IRRESISTIBLE DOCTOR
HER PARTNER'S PASSION
BACK IN HER BED
THE PATIENT DOCTOR*
THE HONOURABLE DOCTOR*

*Country Partners duo

DR DALLORI'S BRIDE

BY
CAROL WOOD

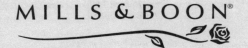

All the characters in this book have no existence outside the imagination of the author, and have no relation whatsoever to anyone bearing the same name or names. They are not even distantly inspired by any individual known or unknown to the author, and all the incidents are pure invention.

All Rights Reserved including the right of reproduction in whole or in part in any form. This edition is published by arrangement with Harlequin Enterprises II B.V. The text of this publication or any part thereof may not be reproduced or transmitted in any form or by any means, electronic or mechanical, including photocopying, recording, storage in an information retrieval system, or otherwise, without the written permission of the publisher.

This book is sold subject to the condition that it shall not, by way of trade or otherwise, be lent, resold, hired out or otherwise circulated without the prior consent of the publisher in any form of binding or cover other than that in which it is published and without a similar condition including this condition being imposed on the subsequent purchaser.

MILLS & BOON and MILLS & BOON with the Rose Device are registered trademarks of the publisher.

First published in Great Britain 2003
Harlequin Mills & Boon Limited,
Eton House, 18-24 Paradise Road, Richmond, Surrey TW9 1SR

© Carol Wood 2003

ISBN 0 263 83439 5

Set in Times Roman 10½ on 11 pt.
03-0403-53889

Printed and bound in Spain
by Litografía Rosés, S.A., Barcelona

PROLOGUE

IGNORING the persistent little niggle under her ribs, Laura glanced in her rear-view mirror and shot flames of annoyance with her eyes at the four-wheel-drive behind her.

Why didn't it overtake? There was plenty of room on the road with no oncoming traffic. But there it was, stuck like a fly in jam a few yards behind her bumper. Laura gritted her teeth, tempted to accelerate. The trouble was, her borrowed sardine-can car would probably give up the ghost there and then if she did.

'Look, you impatient person, you,' she mouthed, her green eyes narrowing under a cloud of tawny hair, 'there's Charbourne Hill. If you don't go past me now, you never will.'

Calculating that she'd have to change down into a rocky second gear that might—or might not—rise to the challenge of the one-in-three gradient ahead, Laura curved the car as close to the verge as she could.

Still the vehicle behind refused to overtake. 'I won't bite,' she muttered into the mirror. 'And I'm not apologizing for the car I'm driving either. I'm driving quite legally and at least I'm not going to cause a major road accident, like some people around here.'

The vehicle, as if in answer, moved out, only to tuck back again. In unison with another sharp twang under her ribs, Laura dropped her foot lightly on the accelerator and braced her stiff shoulders.

Nothing much happened. The car spluttered and gave a polite little backfire, which was mildly embarrassing. But other than that, there was zero response.

'Listen, I'm not asking for miracles. Just get us to the

top of the hill,' she pleaded with the car desperately, 'and we can glide all the way down to Charbourne and still keep our pride.'

Her car gave another rattle and seemed to take heart. Laura tried to sit forward to ease the cramping in her back and wished guiltily that her darling bump was just a bit less rounded. Perhaps it was the way she'd been tensed behind the wheel since leaving London that was causing the little niggles.

That is, she thought suddenly as they ascended the hill, if they *were* niggles.

They could be something else, of course. She *was* eight months pregnant after all. One month to go. And her dates were faultless. There was only one, anyway, and that night would live in her memory for ever.

Laura shook her head a little, tugging at the steering-wheel to keep the car on course. She'd vowed not to give Mark Trevitt a second thought. She'd realised the day he'd refused to take responsibility for their baby that she'd been in love with a fantasy. A man, she had thought, who would love her as much as she loved him. How naïve had she been to think that? Or how foolish? Probably both. The truth was, he didn't deserve one iota of mind space—ever again.

'Ah-h....' Laura heard herself groan. And could hardly believe she had. That seismic little earthquake was definitely more than a niggle. Sweat sprang from her forehead. The car swerved and she only just missed the kerb, or, at least, the hedgerow.

'Breathe,' she told herself calmly. 'In…out… Remember your yoga…'

Easy-peasy, the little voice crowed inside her. You can do anything, Laura Bright. You've told yourself so. You can even give birth while you're driving.

'No, I can't!' she squeaked, and the wheel seemed to spin under her grip. Her palms were damp and the next moment she was fighting to gain control as pain—*real* pain—engulfed her.

The vehicle behind flashed its lights. Laura blinked at it through pain-filled eyes. The mirror seemed misty, or was it her vision? How long had she been trying to ignore this cramping? She had to stop. But where?

She wasn't sure what happened next. Just that everything *did* happen. The contractions, the kick of the baby, the fear and the sheer incredulity. She careered off the road and came to a halt in the hedge.

Laura was vaguely aware she was laying on her back and gazing up at the unfamiliar interior of a car.

'You're OK,' a calm voice said beside her. 'You blacked out for a moment whilst I got you in here.'

'M-my car…'

'It's in much better shape than you,' the man told her wryly as she gazed up into a pair of hauntingly dark eyes. She couldn't tell if they were black or deep brown, but they were huge and fringed with two rows of thick black lashes to die for.

'Wh-where am I?'

'You're in my Jeep. I'm a doctor.' He was propping her head on something soft and as his arms moved across her, he smelt wonderfully of lemons. Or was she delirious? she wondered. The next contraction came quickly and she yelled, desperately needing to push.

'You're about three minutes away from giving birth, so hang in there,' he told her quietly.

Laura reached out and clutched a muscular bicep, her eyes flashing like bright green jewels. The contraction deepened and swept her breath away.

'Your baby's crowning,' he murmured, and she swallowed, trying to remember all the breathing she'd been practising. Tried to remember how to stay relaxed and allow her muscles to work with her.

But the fact was, lying in a strange vehicle on the side

of a hill was a little disconcerting. Her baby was apparently being delivered by a man who said he was a doctor. He appeared to be doing all the right things, but she really couldn't see. And, worst of all, she really didn't care.

All she wanted was for her baby to be born.

'Laura?'

She peered through heavy lids into those eyes again and wondered if she was dreaming. Doctor or not, he was the most gorgeous-looking man and his fingers were weaving gently around her own. 'Laura...if you'll just let go of my arm...'

'S-sorry...'

'That's fine. Now, when the next contraction comes, pant until I tell you to push.'

Without protest, she did as she was told. Besides, what choice did she have but to follow his instructions?

'You're doing fine,' he assured her, and Laura tried to relax before the next contraction. She released her fingers, which had been clamped like glue around his arm, and distantly noted shirtsleeves rolled up and an open collar. The skin below was grainy and tanned and a little cluster of black hair peeped over the white cotton.

Then pain enveloped her and all she could think of was her baby. 'I want to push!' she shrieked, but the stranger shook his head.

'Wait—just a minute...'

'I can't wait!'

'Yes, you can. Good...hold on...well done.' The pause was excruciatingly long and she willed him to speak again.

'OK, Laura, *now* you can push.'

Laura closed her eyes and pushed. It seemed an eternity, it seemed seconds, a brief flash in time, yet a hundred years. Then suddenly she felt the baby emerge and a wonderful feeling of joy filled her.

'One more gentle push,' she heard, and a few seconds later, her baby was born. A lusty wail filled the air as the dark-eyed man held her aloft. Gently he cradled her against his chest and cleared her mouth with tender fingers.

'Well done, Laura. You have a beautiful *bambina*.'

Laura wriggled upward, exhausted but exhilarated. Tears of joy trickled down her cheeks. A daughter, *her* daughter. Her very own. She was here, more beautiful than Laura could ever have imagined.

'Amazing,' Laura heard him whisper, his eyes feasting on the child's crumpled face. Almost reluctantly, it seemed, he lowered her to Laura.

'Oh, my goodness,' Laura breathed as she took her baby in her arms, 'I can't believe it.'

'You had better believe it.' He chuckled as the infant wailed lustily. Laura's heart swelled. The tiny head with a smooth cap of dark hair, the button nose, the clear olive skin and a starfish-like hand which Laura kissed softly. How could she have possibly produced such beauty?

And how sad that Mark had missed such a joy. Would never know what his daughter looked like or sounded like or felt like as she entered this world. A stranger instead had been witness to her birth.

Laura lifted a shaky hand and dragged back her tumble of damp curls. Whatever did she look like? 'I…I don't know what to say. How to thank you.'

The dark-eyed stranger looked as if words failed him too. 'Have you thought of a name?'

She nodded. 'Maria.'

He smiled. It was such a beautiful smile, wide and friendly and his full lips parted expansively over white, even teeth.

'Maria. Yes…she looks like a Maria. Feminine and delicate.'

Laura nodded as she looked down at her baby. 'It was my aunt's name. She brought me up. I called her Aunt M. for short, but now I wish I hadn't. I wish…I wish she was here…' Laura bit her lip, hiding her eyes from the astute stare. It was an emotional moment and he reached forward and touched her arm.

'Let's get you warm,' he said quickly, and rummaged for a cover and draped it over them. 'This is clean and will do until the ambulance comes.'

'I didn't hear you call one,' she said, hugging little Maria.

'You were in shock when I opened your car door. It was clear the baby was on its way.'

Laura nodded slowly. 'I remember looking at the hedge and wondering how I got there.'

He smiled ruefully. 'Yes, so I gathered.'

'I couldn't believe I was having contractions. I'm only just eight months and my dates are right.'

'So you kept telling me. Along with your name—and that you're a nurse. And that you lived in Charbourne once, with your aunt.'

'Did I tell you all that?' Laura croaked. 'How weird. I don't remember a thing.'

'Probably a blessing.' He grinned. 'Because you won't remember my little lecture on your driving either.'

Laura cringed. 'Was it that bad?'

He crinkled a deliciously teasing brow. 'In a word, yes. Next time you get pregnant, I'd advise letting someone else do the driving.'

'Oh, there's not going to be a next time,' Laura said fervently. 'I can't afford more babies.' Then, catching his surprised stare, she realized what she'd said and how it must sound. But before she could speak again, Maria gave another wail.

'Sh-h, little one, you're safe now.'

The man leaned over and pulled up the cover, pausing briefly on the bumps of four small limbs. Then he eased his cramped body backwards, careful to avoid the maternity pack spread out around them.

As a siren sounded in the distance a flutter of warm September wind blew in from the open doors. Laura in-

haled deeply. September would be a very special month
from now on. The air would always taste sweet and these
memories would never fade.

Laura felt a pleasurable wave of sleepiness flow over her.
She curved the cloth down to reveal two little dark studs
that glimmered between folds of silky skin and rosebud lips
blowing bubbles. She kissed the velvet patch on the top of
her baby's head and a sigh of pure joy escaped her.

She finally had her baby and now she could start afresh.

It was many hours later, safely in the maternity wing of
Charbourne General with Maria sleeping contentedly in the
mobile cot beside her bed, that Laura thought about the
events of the day.

A tall, dark stranger had delivered her baby in his car.
This was the driver that had been irritating her for so long,
failing to overtake when there had been plenty of room.
Now she knew why. Her driving must have seemed erratic!

And, if he hadn't rescued her, what would have happened? She might have given birth on the grass verge, in
front of a hundred other passers-by who had cared to glance
idly out of their car windows.

He had also been kind enough to see her off in the ambulance and had promised that he'd arrange to have her car
towed to a garage.

The trouble was, she couldn't remember his name. He
must have told her, but she simply couldn't remember.
Maybe she could find out and thank him. Perhaps the am-
bulancemen would know. Or the nursing staff in A and E
to where she had first been taken.

Laura looked over at Maria and her heart skipped many
beats. The baby was sleeping peacefully in her tiny cot,
unaware of the way she had come into this world. She was
so pretty, with her fragile features and black cap of downy
hair. The same colour as *his*. Ebony.

Suddenly something came back to mind. He'd said one

word. He'd murmured it so softly it had almost passed her by, but she must have remembered it unconsciously.

It rose now in her mind like a bright, twinkling star. His lean, male features had softened as he'd said it and there had been a tender expression in his eyes when he'd murmured…

Bambina.

CHAPTER ONE

*Temporary Practice Nurse required to join friendly, busy
Medical Centre. Apply by telephone or in writing to Julia
Grey, Charbourne Medical Centre, Priory Lane, or call
during daytime hours for appointment.*

LAURA paused on the way to her interview and half
changed her mind. It wasn't a riveting advertisement by
any stretch of the imagination, but she did have her CV
with her and she was only a minute or two away. The odd
thing was, she hadn't intended to stop for a newspaper because Mrs Kent could only have Maria until four and it was
almost two now.

'What to do,' Laura sighed, as she stood under the canopy of the little newsagent a quarter of an hour's walk from
St Helen's Primary. She didn't have an appointment with
the headmistress, but the school secretary had said their
nurse was on sick leave and had hinted they might need a
replacement. It was certainly worth a try.

But the medical centre sounded even more interesting,
and it seemed too good an opportunity to ignore. Laura
picked her way through the lunchtime crowds and paused
at the slim white spear of the clock tower, hoping inspira-
tion would strike. School one way, medical centre the other.

Did she look smart enough to apply to the medical centre? she wondered. Laura glanced in the shop window opposite. She'd dressed carefully, a soft, deep blue linen suit
curving over her slim figure, sheer tights and higher than
normal heels. At five feet eight inches she didn't need the

height but, having lost all her pregnancy weight, it was wonderful to feel reed slim again.

The funky hairclip worked well, too, supporting the thick twist of light brown curls piled high on her head. She'd even splashed out on new underwear. Ridiculous, because no one was going to see it. But the wispy lace bra and daring little thong were a kind of expression of her new self. The new Laura Bright. Mother of Maria. Contender for school nurse at St Helen's—temporary replacement, yes, but, still, it was a job. And a job was what she needed—desperately.

'School it is,' Laura decided, making her way quickly down the narrow street of seaside shops. But when she rounded the corner, a crowd of rather bemused shoppers blocked her path.

'No entry this way,' a policeman was telling them as he arranged a line of orange cones. 'You'll have to go through Priory Lane, I'm afraid.'

'But I only want to get to St Helen's,' Laura protested. 'It's just through the alley there.'

'Sorry, miss. You'll have to go round. The gas board's working in the precinct all day.'

Vague mumbles of complaint echoed through the crowd but everyone moved off and in less than five minutes Laura found herself in Priory Lane. The first building she saw was Charbourne Medical Centre.

It was long and low, with white stucco walls and a smooth pale blue tiled roof. The wide glass doors were open and felt inviting, and Laura ascended the three steps and walked through them into the spacious interior.

'I haven't an appointment,' Laura explained at the reception desk, 'and I'm not registered here. I've come about the practice nurse's post advertised in the *Echo*.'

'You'll need to see Julia, our practice manager,' replied the young receptionist. 'Unfortunately, it's her day off. But I'll make you an appointment for tomorrow if you like.'

Laura paused, running Mrs Kent's busy schedule through

her mind. 'Trouble is, I don't know if my babysitter's free. I've a seven-month-old daughter, you see.'

'I know what that's like,' replied the young woman, identified by her name-badge as Michelle. 'My little boy's at school now, thank goodness.' She paused. 'Could you bring her with you, do you think?'

'I suppose I could...' Laura hesitated. 'But I'd made up my mind to get something settled today. To be honest, I need a job quite quickly.'

Michelle nodded and rolled her eyes. 'I know what you mean. Look, what if I asked one of the doctors if they'd see you?'

'Would you? I mean, aren't they all busy?'

'Well, Dr Saunders and Dr Ray are, yes. Dr Chandra's on her rounds, but Dr Dallori won't mind if he's free. Wait a moment and I'll see.' Michelle twinkled her a smile and disappeared, and Laura strolled over to the waiting area.

It was open plan, furnished with pale blue upholstered bench seats and unusual black-and-white photographs of the harbour. Several patients, reading magazines, sat below a wide, rectangular window that overlooked Clock Tower Street. Soft music played in the background and a cool ripple of air filtered gently around the room. Charbourne Medical Centre was a breath of fresh air compared to the inner-city environment she had been working in.

'Dr Dallori's just finished his surgery,' a voice said behind her, and Laura turned to meet Michelle's friendly blue eyes. 'Go along to the first room on the right.' She lowered her voice and smiled. 'Good luck—and don't be nervous. He's really nice.'

'Thanks.' Laura smiled gratefully and felt a ripple of *déjà vu* as she walked down the corridor. She'd never been to the medical centre before. She hadn't even seen it. After Aunt M.'s death two years ago, she hadn't come back to Charbourne. The agency had taken care of her aunt's guesthouse Sea Breeze and she'd been content to know that the people who were renting it had been satisfactory tenants.

Laura knocked on Dr Dallori's door and her heart rattled like a stone in a bottle as her brain did a series of little flashes—the name Dallori, obviously Italian…

'Come in.'

That was all it took. Two little words. And *his* voice. She'd know it anywhere. Her hand was shaking as she pushed open the door. The man behind the desk looked at her and she gazed wordlessly at him.

'Laura!' he exclaimed, and stood up. 'It *is* Laura, isn't it?'

She nodded, trying to dredge up words that seemed to stick in her throat. 'Dr Dallori…?'

He came towards her, his mouth slanting into a wonderful smile, the same stunning smile that she had thought about so many times since Maria's birth. And now there it was, before her eyes.

If she'd remembered him as being good-looking, she had been wrong. He was out of this world! And she must have been totally delusional if she hadn't realized that last September.

'Laura, this is amazing! I had no idea you were still in Charbourne.'

'I wasn't supposed to be, but Aunt M.'s guest-house didn't sell, so I thought the best thing I could do would be to try to help it on its way…' She came to a full stop again because he was smiling, those eyes staring at her with such disarming beauty that they drove everything else from her mind.

'How is Maria? How are you?'

'We're both fine, thank you. Maria's with a friend for a few hours,' she told him as he pulled out a chair for her and she sat down. 'This is just so strange…' She hesitated. 'I was going to St Helen's Primary and suddenly I find myself here.'

'What were you going to St Helen's for?' he asked as he took his chair.

'A job, hopefully. But then I got diverted by a policeman and a little row of orange cones.'

One smooth eyebrow slid up as he relaxed an elbow on the arm of his chair. 'And you found us instead.'

Laura managed to find her voice despite the pools of ink glimmering across the desk. 'I'd seen your advertisement in the *Echo* and I thought, well, it wouldn't do any harm to enquire. I mean, I really had no idea it was you—and if I had, I probably wouldn't have…' She stopped, realizing what she'd said.

He chuckled and her heart did another little somersault. 'Don't worry, I know what you mean. I'm glad you're here, Laura. We do need a practice nurse whilst Sam is on maternity leave.' He paused, frowning slightly. 'But I'm afraid we couldn't offer you anything longer than September.'

'Perfect.' Laura shrugged. 'Enough time for me to get Sea Breeze straight. You see, after I inherited it from my aunt, I found an agent to handle it in my absence. The last tenant's lease has ended and I've decided to sell. I want to find somewhere to live close to the City.' She took a breath. 'All the place needs is a lick of paint and I'm sure it will fly away.'

He smiled wryly. 'And you intend to give it…this lick by yourself?'

'Oh, yes. I've made a start,' she replied eagerly. 'It's surprising what you can do on a shoestring. Paying out for decorators would cost the earth.'

'Ah, yes, the woman's touch.' He nodded slowly, resting back in his chair, one hand sliding down the black cap of straight dark hair, combed faultlessly to the collar of his grey suit. 'Tell me more about yourself, Laura. I know you grew up here. Where did you train?' His soft, deep voice had her gulping out her story like a five-year-old and she told him everything.

Practically everything. She explained how her parents had died in a car crash when she was seven. How Aunt M. had raised her and how she'd left home to train in London at St Catherine's. She even told him about Shelley and how they'd qualified together and got their first jobs in nursing, renting digs just outside the City.

The one thing she omitted was Mark. The space inside her was too raw, too painful to expose.

'How do you think you'd cope, working in a group practice?' he asked when she'd finished. 'It would be vastly different from a school.'

She nodded thoughtfully. 'Yes, but my coursework was in general nursing and midwifery.'

The dark eyes flickered momentarily as he lifted a pencil, turning it over slowly between his fingers. 'We do have a part-time nurse,' he said thoughtfully. 'Becky works one day a week, though she's been deputizing for Sam. If you were interested in the job, Becky could show you what's involved. Plus, there are refresher courses going on all the time at the college.' He tilted his head. 'How soon could you start, Laura?'

'Well…it's Thursday today,' she faltered, wondering if Mrs Kent would help with Maria. 'Next week?' She added quickly, 'But you haven't seen my CV. You don't really know anything about me.'

'I know enough.' He smiled and she almost stopped breathing. 'Leave your CV with Julia and I'm sure we'll be able to add something positive to it when you leave.'

Laura couldn't believe her luck. He was offering her the job and she'd have it on her CV when she got back to London. 'I don't know what to say,' she murmured breathlessly.

'Yes or no will do.'

'Well, of course—it's yes,' she said quickly.

'And Maria?' he asked hesitantly. 'Is there anyone you can rely on to look after her? It's a four-and-a-half-day week, eight to four-thirty. Quite a commitment.'

'Yes, I know,' she said as he studied her closely. 'But I'm a single parent and the person looking after her today is a neighbour of Aunt M.'s. She's very sweet and I know

I could trust her. She's in her sixties and still runs her little guest-house but I can't rely on her permanently. I'd be happy to pay her, but I think she has enough to cope with already.'

'Yes, I'm sure,' he murmured thoughtfully. 'Have you thought about professional child care?'

Laura shrugged. 'Yes, but I don't know of anywhere…'

'I can recommend the college crèche,' he said, pausing. 'Used by some of our staff. The students come to us, so it's a fair arrangement. Here are the details.' He scribbled on a piece of paper and handed it to her. 'I'll ring in advance if you like—explain the situation.'

'That would be wonderful,' Laura faltered.

'Perhaps you'll be able to get something sorted for Monday.'

Laura nodded, somewhat overwhelmed. She took the paper and slid it into her bag.

'Oh, yes—are you OK for transport?' he asked with a frown.

Laura closed her eyes. 'Heavens, how could I have forgotten? I've never thanked you for what you did for me.'

'Maria was my thanks,' he told her softly. 'To have delivered safely such a beautiful *bambina*.'

There it was, that word again—that Italian accent. And he had a way of saying it, curving his tongue around the syllables like thick, delicious cream.

'I tried to find you,' she protested, ashamed of herself for forgetting. 'But you didn't leave your name on the note you sent up to the ward. And when I went to ask the ambulanceman if he remembered you, he was off duty.'

'I had no idea you went to such trouble,' he told her quietly, a little flicker going across his face.

'But I must pay you for the car,' Laura insisted. 'You had it towed to the garage.'

'No, I drove it,' he told her with a shrug. 'A friend gave me a lift and I managed to get it started. The garage did all the work.'

'Dr Dallori, you've been very kind,' she murmured, and he gave her that stunning smile again.

'You'll more than repay me when you take over Sam's list,' he said as he came to stand beside her. 'Now for the best part. Let me show you around.'

'But aren't you busy?' she asked as she stood up, feeling she'd already taken up too much of his time.

'Not too busy to show off a little,' he told her easily, and Laura wondered if he was always so laid back and charmingly casual. She decided it was his Latin temperament and as she was introduced to the other members of staff, she sensed just how much he was liked and admired.

She managed to concentrate on the guided tour, every now and then losing her concentration as a delicious twang of lemony aftershave drifted past her. It was almost a relief when he returned her to Michelle and left for his next patient. She realized she'd had a full hour of his time, and without an appointment, too.

'Well?' Michelle asked as she made Laura a coffee in the staffroom upstairs. 'I told you he was nice, didn't I?'

Laura nodded as she sat on one of the comfortable easy chairs. 'You'll never believe this, but I've met him before.'

Michelle's blue eyes flew open. 'You're joking.'

'I'm not.'

'Where?'

Laura hid a smile. 'He delivered my little girl.'

Michelle sat down with a thump. 'What, in Charbourne General?'

'No, in his four-wheel-drive.'

Michelle gasped. 'That's incredible.'

'It is, isn't it? I can hardly believe it myself.' Laura filled in the details as Michelle sat open-mouthed. 'The strange thing is, after you left me and I knocked on his door, I had this funny sense of *déjà vu*. And I've never been in here before.'

'You must be psychic.' Michelle giggled.

Laura sipped her coffee and sighed. 'I must have put two

and two together. You know, the name, the dark looks…'
Laura stopped and went red.

'Yummy, you mean,' Michelle sighed.

Laura frowned. 'Imagine being his wife.'

'I have,' Michelle admitted, and they burst into laughter.
Then Michelle lowered her voice to whisper, 'That's the
trouble—he hasn't got one. And all the women fall for
him.'

Laura nodded. 'I can imagine.'

'So, Laura Bright, be warned.'

Laura set down her coffee-cup quickly. 'Oh, don't worry
on my part,' she said firmly. 'I've my little girl to think of.
I'm not looking for involvement. I'm a single mum and I
don't want my life any other way.'

Michelle frowned but asked no more and they washed
their cups and went downstairs for the last part of the tour.
It was almost four by the time Laura left. She was hardly
able to believe she'd be at work on Monday morning.
Tomorrow, though, she would arrange a place at the crèche.

That night she fed Maria and they played beside the fire
in the little sitting room at Sea Breeze, the cosiest of all
the rooms in the eight-bedroomed guest-house. Maria was
teething and her little cheeks were red, and she needed lots
of cuddles.

As Laura held Maria close and kissed the top of her dark,
downy head, her thoughts drifted to Antonio Dallori.

Antonio…

A beautiful name, like all Italian names, created to slide
over the tongue like smooth, rich wine… She murmured it
aloud. 'Antonio…'

Laura shook her head to clear her thoughts. He was
charming, handsome and Italian, a heady cocktail for any
woman. She had been warned.

Well, she didn't need the warning. Those lustrous
Mediterranean eyes said it all. She wondered how many
women had drowned in them.

Laura lifted Maria from her changing mattress on the

floor and took her to her cot in the small boxroom next door.

Maria gave a little gurgle as Laura bent to kiss her.

Bambina, she thought, trying to put all thoughts of Antonio Dallori from her mind. My darling little *bambina*.

Mrs Kent offered to have Maria the following week, but Laura explained about the college crèche.

'Well, if you don't get fixed up, dear,' Mrs Kent replied, 'George and I will have her. We've only got a couple of guests, so it won't be a problem.'

Laura was grateful for Mrs Kent's offer, but the terraced harbourside guest-houses were busy at Easter and she didn't want to burden her neighbour with a young baby. Leaving Maria was difficult enough, but she'd stretched her finances to the limit and so she settled for the crèche.

Added to which, Dr Dallori had said he would alert the college beforehand. A promise he kept, she discovered when she called the next day. To her surprise, she felt her doubts recede as she was shown round the college annexe. The crèche staff were friendly and tried to reassure her, but when Monday came Laura wasn't so confident.

She rose very early to feed and dress Maria and have her things ready, then hugged her tightly. Was this really what she wanted? Was Maria too young at seven months to be left? But when Maria was safely in the car, sitting in her safety seat, blowing bubbles, Laura knew she had to be doing the right thing.

She had a job now. A good one. She could support her child and if this was to be the pattern of her life, she had to make difficult choices.

'We'll take good care of her,' the supervisor assured her as she pushed the buggy into the clean, bright playroom. 'Ring, if you like, at lunchtime and we'll put your mind at rest. It's always a bit worrying on the first day.'

Laura kissed Maria on the cheek, left one of the girls with notes about food and drink and fled. Then she drove to Charbourne, parked in the centre's car park and tried not to think about Maria.

Ten to eight—enough time to find a uniform and do something with her hair. She'd washed it and a waterfall of light brown waves tumbled over her shoulders. She would clip it up and put on a little make-up and hope that she looked as professional as the other staff she'd seen last week.

'How was Maria?' Michelle asked in the cloakroom.

'She was fine,' Laura admitted as she attended to her appearance. 'But I wasn't. I almost changed my mind.'

Michelle nodded sympathetically as she scooped her hair into a ponytail. 'If you think this is bad, wait for her first day at school.'

'How old is your little boy?'

'Almost seven. He's at St Helen's,' Michelle told her, smiling. 'The school you earmarked last week. Glad you came here first?'

'Very.' Laura nodded. 'I'm just nervous.'

'Don't be. Come on, we'll find Becky. Once you're in your uniform you'll feel more confident.'

Becky was in the nurses' room and she wrinkled her nose enviously as Laura tried on the lilac shift with white cuffs and collar.

'How did you get your figure back so quickly?' she asked, frowning down at her own ample curves. 'I put on pounds after my Martin and never seemed to lose them again. Nothing, of course, to do with the chocolate I can't resist.' She giggled, throwing back her crop of short blonde hair.

'I haven't got much of a sweet tooth,' Laura admitted.

'I'm a chocoholic,' Becky said without hesitation. 'Totally addicted. Now, turn around and let me see if it needs taking in. You've got such a teeny waist.'

Laura twirled and Becky nodded. 'Let's just say you're going to make every male head turn in about sixty seconds flat. That shade of lilac goes perfectly with your green eyes.' She looked under her lashes at Laura. 'Michelle said that Dr Dallori delivered your little girl…?'

Laura nodded as she clipped on her name-badge. She'd brought her old one from school and had added the words PRACTICE NURSE. 'I went into labour a month early. He happened to be driving the vehicle behind me and stopped to help.'

'How jammy can you get?' Becky giggled. 'Dr Dallori, of all people.'

Laura nodded. 'Yes, he was very kind.'

'*Kind!*' Becky fluttered her eyes and stared at her. 'That isn't the word I would use. Think scrumptiously gorgeous and you might get close!'

Laura laughed softly. 'Well, yes, I suppose, but—'

At that moment Becky's cheeks went scarlet as she stared over Laura's shoulder. 'Oh, Dr Dallori… Good morning.'

'Hi, Becky…Laura.'

Laura turned on her heel and looked into Antonio Dallori's dark eyes. He was wearing a soft blue linen shirt and flawlessly cut dark trousers and the smell of lemons filled the room as he pushed the door open.

'Hello, Dr Dallori,' Laura said, dredging up her most professional voice. He smiled, his eyes drifting over her slim-fitting dress with obvious approval. 'Becky found you a uniform, I see—and it looks very nice.'

'We aim to please.' Becky chuckled. 'Oh, Dr Dallori, if we need a prescription for an emergency this morning can I ring through?'

'Of course. No problem.' He switched his gaze to Laura again. 'How is Maria? Is she at the crèche or with your neighbour?'

'At the crèche,' Laura replied, aware of Becky's curious stare. She wanted to thank him for his phone call to the college and the influence he must have exerted, but she didn't like to mention it in front of Becky.

'Good,' Antonio Dallori said with a smile that equalled

the warmth in his eyes, and Laura felt the knot tighten in her chest. 'Well, I'll leave you both to get on. And if there's anything I can do to help, let me know. I'm in surgery until midday.'

An unforgettable trail of lemons followed him and gusted back into the room as he closed the door. Becky flopped down in a chair and let out a long sigh. 'If there's anything he can do to help! Where shall I start?'

'He's very—'

'Don't say *kind*, whatever you do,' Becky threatened, wagging a finger.

Laura laughed softly, trying to hide her embarrassment. 'Well, shall we get started?'

'Do you mean to say you can concentrate on work after that?' Becky giggled, leaning forward to turn on the computer. 'Come on, then, let's see what's on the agenda today.'

'What sort of database do we have?' Laura asked, grasping at the opportunity to compose herself as Becky clicked away at the computer.

Becky was right. Antonio Dallori did seem to make an impression on women. But as welcoming as he'd been and, yes, *kind* to help her in the way he had, it could never be anything more.

She didn't want commitment—of any sort, other than to Maria and to her job. She had learnt a painful lesson with Mark. She'd admired him as a teacher and he'd taken advantage of that.

She wasn't embittered, but she had been hurt and at this stage in her life all she wanted was to heal and to start afresh. Maybe when Maria was older... But even then, any friendship would have to balance with Maria's needs. After Mark's deception, there was no way she'd allow her child's happiness to be threatened.

That was why she was here, working to give Maria a future. Out of choice, she wanted to be with her every minute of the day. Out of circumstance, she would never be afforded that privilege. If Mark had loved her...

Laura pulled herself up short. Agonizing over the past was wasted energy. The fact was, he *hadn't* loved her.

'Laura, are you OK?' Becky was staring at her.

Laura forced a smile on her lips. 'Sorry. I was trying to take it all in. We used different software at school.'

Becky shrugged. 'It's like riding a bike. You just need a bit of practice. It's a great system. A bit like the new NHS system, where people without appointments talk to the nurses first on the telephone.'

'And Reception book them in with us instead of a doctor?'

'Yes. If it's something we think we can handle. It's been very successful and our patients seem to like it. But if they need a prescription, of course, we have to ask the doctors.' Becky threw her a mischievous smile. 'Which is absolutely brilliant because that means we can go in to Dr Dallori every five minutes.'

'Really?'

'No.' Becky laughed. 'I wish! You ask whoever is on duty. If it's Dr Collins, you might get growled at or if it's Dr Ray you might have to wait ages, but on the whole it works quite well.'

Laura soon found her feet and by the time the morning was over they had managed to work through a full list. There was nothing that she hadn't been confronted with before, a mixture of sutures, dressings and first aid. And Becky updated her on travel advice and injections.

At lunchtime, Laura reregistered with the surgery. Her own elderly doctor on the outskirts of town was retiring and, anyway, now she worked here, it made sense to be with the centre. Having completed the forms and given them to Michelle, she rang the crèche and held her breath.

'Maria's fine,' the supervisor told her at once. 'She loves

watching the other children. And she's eaten every bit of her lunch.'

Relieved, Laura took her CV to Julia Grey, the practice manager, and introduced herself. Julia was going to eat her lunch in the staffroom and so they went together.

Dr Ravi Chandra came in and sat beside them. They chatted until two when surgery began again, but Laura saw no more of Antonio Dallori.

The afternoon passed quickly as Becky explained the blood-testing procedure. 'You'll be all right tomorrow,' Becky told her confidently. 'There's a couple of ear syringeings and blood-pressure checks. Everything you've done at school.'

'What about emergencies?' Laura asked as she helped Becky replace the equipment on the trolley.

'Oh, you'll have Dr Dallori to help you,' Becky teased, and Laura blushed.

'I hope I won't need help.' Laura shrugged. 'I'd like to be able to cope.'

'Independent little soul, aren't you?' Becky cooed. 'If that was me, I'd be knocking on his door with any excuse. Now, what time do you collect Maria?'

'Half past four.' Laura suddenly felt anxious. It was the longest time she'd ever spent away from Maria.

'You'd better scoot.' Becky waved her away. 'I'll finish up.'

'Are you sure?'

'There's nothing to do, really. Just tidying up and making sure Reception have put all the appointments for tomorrow on computer. I always look because I don't want to be caught with something I'm not prepared for.'

Laura made a mental note to do the same herself in future, but she was grateful to be able to leave on time today. Not even bothering to change her uniform, she gathered her things and ran out to the car park. She was rummaging for her keys in her bag when a little toot made her stop and look up.

A four-wheel-drive was entering the car park and she jumped out of the way. 'Sorry,' she mouthed as it drew to a halt beside her. The window slid down and she found herself gazing up at Antonio Dallori.

'Laura—have you lost something?'

'No, just rummaging for my keys,' she admitted breathlessly. 'Here they are.'

'How was your day?'

'I didn't cause any major catastrophes.' She laughed softly, wondering if his eyes were really black or very dark brown.

'I'm sure you didn't.'

She moved slightly. 'I'm sorry. I have to rush. I said I'd be at the crèche for four-thirty.'

'Drive carefully,' he warned, hiking up an eyebrow and she laughed softly. 'See you tomorrow.'

Laura hurried on, tugging the zip across her shoulder-bag, conscious of the drumming of the diesel engine as he parked. He waved as she drove out of the car park and she fought to keep her eyes from glancing in the rear-view mirror. What she needed now was to go home with Maria and forget everything that happened today, including Antonio Dallori.

'Your little girl's a star,' the supervisor told Laura when she arrived. Maria blew bubbles at her from her nest in the buggy. 'Such a happy little thing.'

'She is, isn't she?' Laura said proudly, her heart finally settling back to its normal rhythm as she bent down to brush a kiss on Maria's cheek.

Maria continued to gurgle all the way home and Laura felt confident the crèche was a good place for her to be. All she had to do now was spend as much time with her baby as she could to make up for her absence during the day.

Laura was deep in thought as she drove. She might even be able to save a little money after she'd paid the crèche fees and the rest of the bills. She was so absorbed with her sums that she didn't notice the tall figure leaning casually over the harbour wall close to Sea Breeze.

It was only as she parked that she saw him. He was almost in silhouette, with the sun splintering behind him. He had been gazing out over the still blue water and now the sunshine profiled his strong, classical features.

Then, with the ease of some exotic wild animal, Antonio straightened and began to walk across the road towards her.

CHAPTER TWO

'HI, THERE,' Antonio said as he neared, and Laura felt her heart slam.

She couldn't think why he was there, but a dozen awful possibilities flew into her mind. Maybe she hadn't got it right today. Had one of the patients complained? Perhaps the elderly lady who had protested that her blood pressure couldn't have shot up and that it was Laura's mistake. She'd taken it again and it had been exactly the same, but perhaps she still hadn't been happy.

'Has something happened at surgery?' she asked anxiously.

'No, but I found this in the car park.' He delved in his pocket and brought out her purse. 'I'd forgotten my mobile and on my way back in to get it, I found your purse.'

'Goodness! I hadn't even realized I'd lost it.'

'It was where we stopped to talk,' he told her. 'I tried phoning you, but there was no reply so I thought it was just as easy to call by.'

Laura shook her head wordlessly. 'I was in such a rush to see Maria and looking for my keys...'

'Ah, Maria,' he murmured, stooping to peer in the back of the car. 'Did she have a good day?'

'Yes, apparently.' The breeze from the sea curled softly around them. The sun was still shining and the April sky was filled with little clouds that looked like polka dots. Laura found herself gazing at the back of his head and his thick straight hair, comparing its faultless ebony to the silver grey of his suit. The wide shoulders strained at the clearly expensive cloth, the ripples falling elegantly away as he straightened up.

Laura didn't know what to do. He'd found her purse and had taken the trouble to bring it to her. It seemed rude not to offer at least a cup of tea. 'I always seem to be in your debt,' she faltered.

'Quite the reverse,' he assured her, straightening up and flashing her a wide white smile.

She wasn't certain what he meant, but then Maria gave a little wail and she said quickly, 'Would you like a cup of tea? Coffee? Or something cool? I just have to bring in the buggy and my things.'

'Can I help?' he offered at once. 'Is the boot open?'

Before she could speak he'd gone round and opened it, just as Maria began to make soft mewing sounds. 'It's all right, darling, we'll soon be in and settled,' Laura whispered as she dived into the back of the car and unfastened her. She gave Maria the biggest of hugs, kissed her head and grabbed her bags from the passenger seat.

She had missed her daughter so much. And yet Maria seemed none the worse for her day. Carrying Maria and her bags to the front door, Laura slid her key in the lock. A faintly musty smell oozed out, but it was much better than it had been when she'd first arrived. Now there were homely cooking aromas and the smell of new paint and an indefinable scent of child.

Laura turned and watched Antonio attempting the puzzle of putting the buggy together. She smiled as she watched him, his tall figure hunkering down as he carefully pushed back the hood and slipped the buggy into safety mode.

Pretty good for a beginner, Laura thought, then wondered if he was, in fact, a beginner. She didn't know anything about him. He might have children or even a secret wife somewhere, the little voice inside her head shrieking—yes, just like Mark. So she hurried in, down the long, newly emulsioned hall to the kitchen and hoped to goodness he wouldn't take her up on that cup of tea.

There was no way she wanted the slightest involvement, Laura reminded herself sternly. She was determined to keep this relationship impersonal. All because of one weak moment, her darling child had come into the world. Not that she regretted Maria. She was the best thing that had ever happened to her. But being fatherless and ignored wasn't the birthright she would she have chosen for her daughter.

'Would you like me to hold her for a while?' a deep voice asked as Laura tried to juggle her bags onto the table.

She gazed up into a pair of hypnotically dark eyes and didn't protest as his long, tanned fingers grasped Maria carefully, skirting her waist and supporting her tiny back. Very slowly he cocooned her against him, whispering softly as he rocked her.

For a moment Laura couldn't move. She was transfixed by the sight of her tiny daughter in this man's arms. He seemed to be entirely unaware of her gaze as he lifted the minuscule hand locked to his index finger and Maria gave a heart-stopping mew of…could it really be recognition?

Antonio made himself comfortable in the carver chair by the ancient pine table. Maria curled up in his arms, fascinated by the dark, handsome features, her little murmurs doing something extraordinary to Laura's insides as she made tea.

Everything seemed so normal, Laura thought as Mrs Kent's fat tabby cat shrank itself through the cat flap and curled herself at a pair of well-shod male feet. No change even in the golden beams of a sinking sun, casting hazy ladders of light onto the table surface. Neither was there any difference in the hiss of the boiler or the creaking of the plumbing or the call of gulls through the open window.

Yet nothing was normal, she realized. There was a stranger sitting in Aunt M.'s high-backed carver chair, his long legs stretched out, seeming to be at ease with everything around him. His deep laughter was trickling through her bones like honey and she fought against it. She didn't want to feel like this. So vulnerable!

She didn't *need* a man in her life. She was coping perfectly without one and she would do well to remember that.

'Her eyes are the same colour,' he said quietly, as he glanced up at Laura. 'They are a deep greeny gold, like yours. Or perhaps a shade deeper.'

Had he really noticed the colour of her eyes? 'I don't suppose they'll stay the same,' she said dismissively.

'Oh, I think they will.' He gazed back at Maria, propped comfortably on his long thigh, gazing up in silent adoration. 'You're teething, little one, aren't you?' He smoothed the red patches that had appeared on Maria's cheeks with a tender finger. 'The sooner those pretty pearls appear, the better.'

It was almost painful to watch Maria's response as she sucked gummily on her non-existent teeth. There seemed to be some strange bond—but that was impossible, Laura decided, shaking her head a little. 'You haven't drunk your tea,' she said stiffly, suddenly needing her own space.

'Oh, yes.' The murmured words were lost as Maria's shrill little cry echoed through the high-ceilinged kitchen. 'She's hungry. I'd better feed her.'

Antonio looked round as if he'd suddenly realized where he was. 'Of course you must. Here…' He rose slowly, peeling Maria from his chest and depositing her gently in Laura's arms. Laura held her protectively, refusing to look up and into the dark, watchful gaze.

'I'm sorry. I've delayed you,' he said after a while, in cool tones that mirrored Laura's.

'It's all right,' Laura replied, wishing he'd go. He was too much of a distraction. And he made her think of things she shouldn't be thinking about. 'It's just that I want to get her into a routine. I'll have to, if I'm working. It's best for both of us.'

He nodded slowly, his eyes finding Maria again. He smiled softly and Laura's senses swam. 'Do you know what today is, Laura?' he asked, glancing at her with hypnotic black eyes.

She frowned. 'The first of April.'

'We say in Italian *Pesce d'Aprile*. A special day, a surprise day. And for me today was a very wonderful surprise. I have seen your *bambina* again.'

Laura thought her heart had stopped beating as his eyes met hers in an unspoken message. But she was too frightened to translate it. Her trust in human nature would never be the same after Mark and she would be a fool to think otherwise.

'Goodnight, Laura,' he said, turning quietly to leave the kitchen. As the front door clicked, silence filled the room and only the smell of lemons lingered faintly in the air.

As worried as she may have been about leaving Maria, Laura enjoyed her first week at the medical centre more than she'd thought possible. There was a fulfilment to her work that motherhood had overshadowed. In the days that followed her return to nursing, she realized just how much she had missed the work.

By the end of the week, she had taken two full days by herself. She'd found little that she hadn't been able to handle. Those patients who'd needed prescriptions she'd referred to the doctors, but there hadn't been many. And all of them had been delighted to meet her.

'I may as well not come in next week,' Becky teased on Friday afternoon. 'You don't need me here at all.'

Laura smiled but her green eyes were faintly doubtful. 'I was just lucky.'

'Lucky?' Becky grimaced. 'What about Mrs Frost on Tuesday, then? There's practically no one here who fancies seeing her. She's always a problem, but you dealt with her and off she went, happy as a lark.'

'She only needed reassurance. Her diabetes makes her irritable. And I'm new, so she enjoyed telling me all about it.'

'Well, whatever, but the girls on Reception breathed a sigh of relief. She monopolises them sometimes. But she tottered off quite happily on Tuesday.'

'Do we have any clinics planned for next week?' Laura asked.

'On Wednesday we've got the antenatal run by our midwife, Mo Fielding. If you want to look in, I'll be here for the routine stuff.' Becky inclined her head. 'Anything exciting planned for Easter?'

'Spending time with Maria.' Laura smiled. 'I hope it's good weather.'

'Forecast's OK. Anyway, we're almost finished here. One more to come, a tetanus. Someone by the name of Mitchell Fraser.' She hesitated. 'Could I ask a favour? I need to top up the freezer before school breaks up. Would you mind if I left you to it?'

'Of course not.' Laura shrugged. 'Off you go. See you Monday.'

'Great,' Becky said, grabbing her bag. 'Have a good weekend.'

After she'd gone, Laura sat down to familiarise herself with the medical history of her next patient. But before she'd gone very far there was a knock at the open door.

Antonio stood there, dressed in a navy blue polo shirt and sleek dark trousers. He smiled that wide white smile that made her heart do somersaults and she took a breath.

'Becky's not here, I'm afraid,' she told him quickly.

He nodded, coming in and sinking down into the chair next to the desk. 'I wonder if I can enlist your help. You'll be seeing Mitchell Fraser for a tetanus?'

She nodded. 'Yes. Is there a problem?'

'I don't know yet. He came to me before going on holiday, asking for painkillers. He said he'd pulled a muscle in his back. But I had my doubts and sent him for blood tests.' He handed the results to her. 'As you can see, his gamma G and urea are raised, which confirms my suspicions that his trouble is kidney- and liver-related. However, when he asked me why I wanted the tests done and I explained, he told me I was talking rubbish.'

'Oh,' Laura sighed. 'That's difficult.'

'Quite frankly, I'm a little surprised he actually followed through with the tests. Anyway, I've told Reception to send him to me before he has the tetanus.'

'So...' Laura murmured uncertainly, 'where do I come in?'

Antonio lifted his eyes. 'I don't think he'll take kindly to what I have to say. The tests suggest an alcohol issue and, no doubt, he'll resent any advice I give him. I'd like to know if there's any reaction. It may help with future treatment.'

'But he might say nothing,' Laura protested uneasily. 'After all, it's just a jab he's coming in for.'

'I know. But I'd still like to know what you think afterwards.'

She was a little mystified. This would be the first time she'd ever met Mitchell Fraser, so she could hardly make any health judgements and she felt slightly uneasy about her role in all this. But she couldn't really refuse so she nodded and was rewarded with a smile that made her tummy scramble.

'I'll do my best,' she agreed reluctantly. 'But I'm not sure it will be much.'

'Good. Speak to you later,' he murmured, but when he reached the door he looked back, a dark eyebrow quirking up. 'Any sign of those little pearls yet?'

At first she didn't understand what he meant. Then she remembered what he'd said as he'd held Maria in his arms. 'Two teeth,' she said, as colour poured into her cheeks. 'Just peeping through.'

'Ah,' he said softly, and threw her one last glance.

She managed—just—to meet that piercing gaze before he closed the door quietly behind him. It took her a full five minutes to recover. Idiot, she told herself crossly. You're overreacting. Blushing like a teenager and thinking he really does care about Maria.

Which is exactly what you don't want, Laura Bright. It's just too dangerous to get involved. Haven't you learnt your lesson by now?

A long sigh left her lungs and she focused on the computer screen, running her eyes over Mitchell Fraser's details. Forty-eight, a restaurateur and club owner. Thrice divorced, signed on two years ago as a temporary resident and now a patient registered with Dr Dallori. Other than that—nothing!

What if the man sat there in total silence and never volunteered a word? What if he talked about everything under the sun except his health? And why, anyway, did Antonio want her help?

She was debating this question when Joanne, the receptionist on duty, rang through. 'Mr Fraser's just gone in to Dr Dallori, Laura. Then he's coming in for his tetanus, OK?'

'Thanks, Joanne.' Laura sat thoughtfully back in her chair. Was she being given some kind of test here? And if so, why? Did Antonio doubt her competence or was it, heaven forbid, a little pique at her coolness on Monday?

She'd been polite enough, but she'd been firm, too, and had made it plain it had been time for him to leave. But surely he couldn't have taken exception to that?

Laura felt the first little wave of anxiety. She hoped she was wrong, but did Antonio possess an ego that couldn't take rejection?

She sat there, turning the possibilities over in her mind, then stood up and began to prepare the trolley, wondering how she was going to handle the situation.

Mitchell Fraser was tall, with luxurious blond hair swept back from his forehead, and he was smiling when he came in, exuding an air of casual confidence. But there was a slightly unnatural flush about his face and tiny broken veins had begun to seed themselves around his nose and light grey eyes.

The man had charm, she had to admit. He reached for her hand before he sat down and held it just a fraction too long. Laura withdrew her fingers and smiled. With the preliminaries over, he removed his jacket and she administered the tetanus injection. If she'd had any concern about her patient not communicating, she had worried unnecessarily as afterwards he made himself comfortable in the chair.

'I've just seen the doctor,' he told her with a shrug. 'He seems to think I might have a problem with my health.'

'In what way?' Laura asked.

'Well, I'm as fit as a fiddle. I told him so. In fact, I only came today for the tetanus. I trod on something on the beach last night. I keep a boat and we had a little party and a bit of a swim. As I said, I like to keep fit. So I think the doctor has got it all wrong.'

Laura wondered about the partying and swimming and in which order they had come. But she said nothing and Mitchell frowned at her.

'What, no lecture?' he gasped theatrically.

'I'm sure Dr Dallori has explained everything to you,' she said firmly.

'Yes, but I never asked for these...*tests* in the first place. I pulled a muscle and that's all it was.'

'So the pain has disappeared?' Laura asked.

This question brought about the first real hesitation from Mitchell. 'More or less,' he replied indifferently. 'Muscle pulls often take a while to mend. I know that because I work out in the gym and it's happened to me before. To accuse me of practically being an alcoholic—'

'I'm sure that wasn't the case, Mr Fraser,' Laura interrupted. 'It's the doctor's duty to explain the tests, which are normally quite reliable. They explain how, when the action of the kidneys is inhibited, stones can form and the related pain is a warning sign. Similarly the gamma, when raised, provides a guide to the level of alcohol intake.'

'Well, he's done his duty,' Mitchell said, rising to his feet, 'and so have you. But I've got a business to run and time is pressing. Thank you for your concern and I'm grateful. Nevertheless, I won't be bothering you again.'

'It's no bother to see you,' Laura said evenly. She said no more, thinking she might do more damage than good if she did. He shook her hand again and left, and Laura watched him from her window overlooking the car park.

He drove a luxurious car that looked as if it could eat up the road and the man behind the wheel was someone who obviously took his health problems lightly. So lightly, in fact, he was quite convincing in his argument that he was fit. However, test results rarely lied.

When she had cleared away, she realized it was almost four o'clock and that she had better speak to Antonio before she left. She hurried along the hall and his door was ajar. She knocked and he called for her to come in.

'Oh, Laura, can you give me five minutes?' he asked as she entered.

She stopped abruptly, her eyes meeting those of his patient seated in the chair.

'I'm sorry, I didn't know you were busy,' she apologized.

'I won't be long.' He smiled and Laura nodded and made a quick exit.

Back in her room, she waited for five minutes, which turned into ten. Then fifteen. She couldn't stay any longer, she decided, and when she left surgery, he was still in his room. So she left a message with Joanne, offering her apologies, but saying that she had to leave.

Oddly, the drive to the crèche went almost without her knowing it. When Laura thought about it later, she realized it had been one of those occasions that had slipped by so swiftly she hardly recalled leaving the centre.

She had been preoccupied and she knew why. She had been thinking about the young woman sitting in the chair by Antonio's desk. Dark-haired, slender and very attractive, she'd turned briefly to meet Laura's gaze. Laura didn't know what it was, but at that moment a knot tightened unpleasantly under her ribs.

'Good weekend?' Becky asked on Monday.

'Mmm. It was so warm we were out most of the time.' Laura nodded, straightening her uniform as they looked in the cloakroom mirror.

'You live by the harbour, don't you? Is it one of those quaint old places by the sea wall?' Becky leaned forward to study her reflection, brushing her short blonde bob behind her ear.

'Quaint being the operative word,' Laura replied. 'I grew up there, but after my aunt's death an agency let it out for me. Then I decided to sell it and now I'm trying to decorate some of the scruffier rooms.'

'Wow, come round to my house some time.' Becky rolled her eyes. 'Barry hasn't got a clue. Well, he has, just pretends he hasn't to get out of it.'

'Oh, my skills only go as far as a coat of paint,' Laura admitted. 'I'm no great shakes with woodwork or anything.'

'By the way,' Becky said as she glanced at her watch, 'there's a staff meeting tonight. We're invited.'

'Oh, dear, I don't know,' Laura hesitated. 'It's Maria. I suppose I could ask Mrs Kent—'

'Don't worry,' Becky shrugged. 'As long as one of us is there. I'll fill you in. Oh, by the way, Dr D. left a note on the desk. For you.'

'For me?' Laura felt her cheeks burn as Becky raised her eyebrows.

'I found it when I went in there this morning, propped against the computer.'

Laura scooped her hair into a band and then walked to the door, with Becky following behind her.

'He says he's sorry he missed you on Friday night,' Becky said as they went along the hall and into the nurses' room. 'You are a dark horse, Laura Bright. Thought you were off men. Obviously not this particular one, though.'

'Becky, it's nothing of the sort. I just…' Laura began as she picked up the piece of paper and scanned its contents.

'Go for it, girl, that's what I say,' Becky said, peering at the note.

'Becky, it's about a patient, that's all.'

'Well, look.' Becky jabbed the note. 'He does say he'll catch up with you.' Becky widened her eyes dramatically. 'The thing is, are you willing to be caught?'

'Oh, Becky, stop it.' Laura laughed lightly as she slid the note in her pocket. 'It's nothing to do with what you're thinking.'

'I'm not thinking anything,' Becky said innocently.

'It's about someone I saw last week. Dr Dallori said he…' She stopped, reluctant to go into details as Becky would wonder why Antonio had enlisted her help and she'd jump to all the wrong conclusions. 'Well, he just wanted an update, that's all.'

'Eager beaver.' Becky sniffed, and Laura could tell she was a little put out. Luckily Dr Chandra came in at that moment and asked if one of them could see a patient who needed ulcer dressings changed.

'Send her in, Dr Chandra,' Becky said. 'One of us will do it.'

As Dr Chandra left, Dr Saunders, the young locum that

had been with the centre since Christmas, asked for help with an ECG.

Becky volunteered and Laura was left to see Dr Chandra's patient. She breathed a sigh of relief. Becky was sweet but Laura recalled with a shiver how easily things could get misconstrued in a small community. There was no way on earth she was going to have it happen to her twice. Finding out like she had about Mark had made her realize how cruel gossip could be.

Happy with his fresh, comfortable dressings and a lively chat, the elderly man left. Then Reception slotted in two emergencies, chest infections that Laura asked Dr Ray and Dr Collins to see. It was midday by the time Becky skidded round the door, out of breath and flushed.

'Sorry I had to leave you,' she sighed heavily. 'The ECG machine had an off day, and I hung on to make sure Dr Saunders was OK. He asked me to help with another couple of patients—have you been all right?'

'Fine.' Laura shrugged.

'Oh, and I bumped into lover-boy as I was coming back.'

'Who?' Laura asked frowningly.

'Dr D., of course!'

Laura's heart sank like a stone. 'Oh.'

'Guess what? He said to tell you he'll see you later but he has to go out on calls.' Becky rolled her eyes.

Laura tried to make light of it. 'Well, there you are. It's nothing important. Now, I must just go to the cloakroom.' And without giving Becky a chance to ask more, she fled.

Luckily it was a hectic afternoon and Becky seemed to forget about Antonio. She wasn't in the room when Laura saw him striding across the car park to his vehicle, and by four-fifteen it was time to leave and she made a dash to her car.

Maria was grizzling when she collected her from the crèche and Laura thought it was probably more teeth on

the way. The following day she was still irritable and Laura
wondered if she might be coming down with a cold.

It was Becky's day off and Laura took her surgery alone.
She didn't see much of Antonio either, just a glimpse of
him in the office talking to one of the staff. Laura decided
that fate might be kind to her and he'd forget about Mitchell
Fraser, which would in turn let her off the hook with Becky.

On Wednesday, there was the antenatal clinic and Becky
introduced Laura to the midwife, Mo Fielding. Laura enjoyed talking to the mums so much she lost track of time
and had to dash for Maria. Her little cheeks were pink and
she had a fitful night's sleep. And on Thursday, she was
irritable again, with more little pink splodges on her cheeks.

'It must be teeth,' Laura sighed as she handed her over
to Sue Kemp, the supervisor.

'Don't worry, I'll ring you if there's a problem,' Sue told
her.

But Laura did worry and when Sue rang at one o'clock,
all her nerve ends jumped to attention.

'She needs a cuddle,' Sue said regretfully. 'I'm sure it's
teeth. But only Mum will do.'

'I'll come straight over,' Laura said, her heart lurching.

'Away with you,' Becky told her when Laura explained.
'We haven't much on anyway. Everyone's in holiday mood
now. Hot cross buns and Easter eggs and all that.'

'I'm sorry,' Laura apologized, grabbing her things. 'I
owe you.'

'You most certainly do,' Becky teased. 'Oh, by the way,
Dr Collins is on call if you need him. He's covering until
Saturday evening. So if you're worried about Maria, just
give him a bell. He's really good with kids, too.'

Laura nodded. 'Thanks, Becky. I hope I won't have to.'
But when she collected Maria and took her home, her
daughter's cheeks were burning and there was a hint of a
rash.

Laura was awake most of the night and so was Maria.

In the morning, she had a raised temperature and Laura rang the surgery. It was Good Friday, but she could drive in if they wanted her to. But the answering service took the symptoms and seconds later someone rang her back to say the doctor would call.

Laura waited anxiously, rocking Maria in her arms. The moments ticked by and Maria became a hot little coal in her arms. Laura felt lonelier than she had ever felt in her life. Lonelier even than when Mark had told her he was married. Even when he'd said he could never love her. And now the loneliness was mixed with desperation.

When the doorbell rang, she laid Maria in her cot and hurried to answer it. But it wasn't Dr Collins who stood there. It was Antonio Dallori.

CHAPTER THREE

'I THOUGHT you were Dr Collins,' Laura said in a voice that didn't sound like her own. High-pitched and quavering, it seemed like a hollow echo bouncing from the walls. She pushed back the tangle of light brown curls falling around her face, knowing she looked a total mess.

A total wreck, more accurately.

She'd hardly recognized herself in the mirror this morning. Her eyes were the colour of pale gooseberries, peering out from dark sockets. Her paint-spattered jeans and shirt were the first clothes she'd scrambled into at some unearthly hour in the night. And other than managing to brush her teeth, she hadn't even put a flannel to her face.

'Jamie's out on an emergency,' Antonio told her calmly as he came in. 'I happened to be in the surgery, looking for some papers, when your call came through.'

'I'm sorry to bring you out,' she apologized, closing the door and trying to compose herself. 'I would have driven in. Perhaps I should have and maybe I'm overreacting...' She stopped, taking a breath and biting her bottom lip. 'I've just been so worried.'

At once he lowered his case to the floor and reached out, his big hands gently cupping her shoulders. 'Hey, it's OK. Tell me—slowly—what's happened.'

'I should have known she wasn't well,' Laura burst out. 'I thought it was her teeth, that there were more to come after those two bottom ones. I should have kept her home yesterday, but I took her to the crèche and—'

'Has she a temperature?' he broke in, and she nodded.

'There's a rash, too,' she said heavily, looking away. She didn't want him to see the fear in her eyes.

'Where?'

'On her cheeks and a few spots on her chest.' As she said this, she seemed to collapse inside. 'I'm sorry,' she apologized again. 'I don't seem to be handling this very well. So many things go through your mind.'

'I know,' he said quietly, 'but it's rarely ever one of them. When did you first notice she wasn't right?'

Laura tried to think. 'On Tuesday, I think. She was irritable and grizzling and not at all like herself. Then yesterday Sue phoned me from the crèche. I went in and collected her, and last night I found the rash.'

He smiled, squeezing her arms gently. 'OK, let's have a look, shall we?'

Her legs felt like cotton wool as she led the way to the flat at the back. Maria's door was open. The room was chaotic. She hadn't put away the sofa bed that she'd tried to sleep on and the toys were in a muddle.

'You've had a rough night,' he said, and Laura nodded as they walked over to the cot. 'Is she eating?'

'No, she really didn't want her bottle either.' Laura bent over and lifted Maria into her arms. She was about to suggest they go into the other room, but he was already scooping up the bed linen and stacking everything on top of a cupboard. With a flourish he returned the sofa bed to normal and patted the pale green cushions into place.

Then he steered her over and gently pushed her down. He sat beside her, his long legs outstretched, the faded jeans clinging to his thighs and a loose shirt lapping over his belt. He smelt deliciously fresh and the neck of his shirt was open, the top buttons undone. She looked at the grainy, dark skin and her heart took a leap as his arm brushed hers.

'Hello, little one.' He smiled, his dark eyes focused on Maria. She wasn't crying but chewing her gums with a crumpled expression that made Laura's heart ache. Two bright clown's patches dotted her cheeks.

'Do you remember me?' he asked, threading a finger through the clenched little fist.

To Laura's astonishment, Maria offered a wobbly grin. He laughed softly. 'I hope that's a yes.'

'She hasn't smiled in days,' Laura sighed.

'She has her *mamma*'s beautiful smile,' he said and with his free hand flipped open his case. 'Now, shall we take off her vest?'

Trying to ignore the compliment she thought she'd just heard, Laura drew the thin cotton vest over Maria's head. She'd lost count of the times in the night she'd changed her daughter's clothing, sponging her down and trying to reduce her fever. Nothing had seemed to help.

'Temperature first, then her chest,' he said quietly, and slid the bulbous end of the thermometer under Maria's arm. Three long minutes later, he removed it and placed the stethoscope to her chest.

'No rattles,' he murmured, 'but her temperature's raised a bit. Now, let's have a look at this rash.'

Laura's heart beat heavily. Every mother worried over her baby, she knew that. And she tried to tell herself that a rash and fever didn't necessarily add up to something dreadful. But as she watched the dark gaze go over her child, the minutes seemed to be endless.

'She's had all her routine immunizations?' he asked as he frowned at the bright red rash on Maria's tummy.

'Yes, at the hospital clinic. Her last check was with the paediatric neurologist and developmental paediatrician.'

'Because Maria was premature?'

'Yes. They wanted to check her motor skills.'

'Which are, of course, quite perfect,' he commented, lifting Maria's little hand. She clung to it, giving him a long and silent stare. 'Those two little teeth have been responsible for much,' he sighed. 'But not for this rash.'

'So, if it's nothing to do with her teeth,' Laura asked anxiously, 'what is it?'

He was silent for a moment, then looked up. 'Can't you guess?'

She shook her head numbly. 'No.'

'Forget the rash on her chest. Concentrate on her cheeks. What does the rash look like?'

Laura thought for a moment. She had gone through just about everything in her mind, from heat rash to meningitis. Then she looked at Maria's cheeks again and gave a little gasp. 'It's not…*fifth*, is it?'

He smiled. 'Known better as slapped-cheek.'

'Because it's just as if the child has been slapped!' Laura gasped incredulously. 'But she's just a baby. And babies don't get it—do they?'

'Fifth or erythema infectiosum is uncommon in babies, that's true,' he agreed.

'And so it's nothing to worry about?'

He shook his head. 'The infection, like a common cold, will clear of its own accord. She'll need rest, plenty of fluids and once the spots appear over the rest of her body, she'll start to feel better.'

Laura shook her head slowly. 'I've seen toddlers and young children with it, but never a baby.'

'That's because babies are usually protected by antibodies in the womb,' he nodded. 'But we must remember Maria is nearly eight months old.'

Relief flowed through every bone in her body. 'I'm a nurse,' she fretted. 'I should have known.'

'You're also a mother and that instinct is the strongest. You are too subjective. It's easy to overlook the obvious.'

Laura closed her eyes, expelling a sigh. She couldn't believe that she hadn't spotted the clear markings of such an unmistakable infection.

When at last she opened her eyes he was gazing at her. In the morning light she could see how beautiful his eyes were. The deepest of browns, fringed by thick black lashes that looked like little fans as they swept his cheeks. They were so huge and deep that she felt that if she let go of her control for a few seconds she might drown in them.

'I thought of all the wrong things,' she admitted, dragging her gaze down to Maria. She was asleep, curled contentedly in her arms. 'I had to keep telling myself she hadn't had any fits or seizures. And when I pressed a glass against her spots, they faded. So it couldn't be meningitis. But my imagination still went into overdrive. All my training and experience vanished. I felt so helpless in the night.'

'I wish I could have helped you,' he said softly, and a little flicker went across his face. Then he cleared his throat and looked down at Maria. 'She's making up for the sleep she's lost. Did *you* sleep last night?' he asked after a moment.

'Not much really.'

'And the night before?'

'Catnaps, I suppose.'

'Which probably means you've been sleep-deprived for forty-eight hours,' he pointed out. 'Don't you think you should do something about that?'

She nodded. 'I'll sleep when you've gone.'

He smiled ruefully. 'I'm sorry. But I have difficulty in believing that.'

She met his eyes and felt colour flood her cheeks. He was right. She wouldn't sleep until Maria was better and she'd probably spend all day living on her nerve ends.

'Don't tell me to try to sleep,' she pleaded. 'I couldn't, really. Not until her temperature's down at least.'

'I've nothing to do for the rest of the day.' He shrugged easily. 'I'll stay if you want to catch up with a few hours.'

'But I couldn't expect you to,' she protested, horrified. 'You're not even supposed to be working.'

'It's because you have no expectations, Laura,' he said quietly, 'that I'm happy to be here. For your daughter's sake, I think you must consider my offer.'

Laura looked at him, trying to think of a reasonable argument. She knew what he was saying made sense. She knew she was exhausted but that she wouldn't sleep a wink until Maria improved. Even if she pulled out the sofa bed and lay beside the cot, she would lie awake, listening. But how could she accept his help yet again?

'Dr Dallori—' she began, but he stopped her.

'Antonio, *please*.'

She lifted her shoulders. 'I can't call you that.'

'Away from the practice you can.' He paused, crooking an eyebrow. 'So you'll do as I suggest and rest for your little girl's sake?'

He was making it easy for her. And she had no energy left to argue. If she had to leave Maria in someone's care, who better than a doctor?

'You'll wake me after lunch?' she asked doubtfully.

He nodded, his eyes locking with hers, then he lifted Maria carefully from her arms, laid her in the cot and tucked the sheet over her. Pausing to see that she was still asleep, he gave a little nod of satisfaction and turned round. 'Now, your turn,' he said with a grin, and stretched out his hand.

She found herself taking it and being led out of the room and into the hall. 'Which way?' he asked, and she nodded to her right. He led her into the small bedroom next to Maria's, tugged her firmly to the bed and sat her down.

'All you have to do is close your eyes,' he instructed, 'and turn your mind off everything.'

'I don't know if I can,' she whispered, already missing the strong comfort of his hand and hating herself for her weakness.

'You will,' he assured her.

She nodded obediently, feeling self-conscious under his gaze. She thought for a horrible moment he was going to wait to see if she undressed and got into bed. But he must have sensed her thoughts as he smiled and walked to the door.

'Maria's bottle is in the fridge,' she called, 'and her strained food is there, too.'

He nodded and mouthed, 'Sleep.'

The door clicked behind him and she sat quite still, almost too weary to take off her clothes. But a few minutes later she lay under the sheet, listening to the unfamiliar noises in the house, all her troubles melting away.

Maria was going to get better. Her little girl would recover. And somebody she could rely on was watching over her as she slept.

Had he really held her hand and led her to the bedroom? Or had she imagined it? But she couldn't have done—there were quiet movements in the hall outside and a soft footfall to prove it. So it hadn't all been a dream. And she really could allow herself to rest for a few hours.

Slowly her eyelids fluttered down, her palm still tingling from where it had been pressed against his, and she fell into a deep and peaceful sleep.

The smell of something cooking woke Laura. Or at least that's what she thought it was. Her eyes opened slowly, registering the darkened room and the muffled sounds outside. With a start she remembered a few vague details of what had gone on. But the overriding sense of apprehension made her sit up too quickly and her heart beat a tattoo.

Then it all fell into place, the missing pieces slotting together, and she lay against the pillows, letting it all flow back. Maria didn't have some frightening disease. All her worst fears were ungrounded. And Maria's recovery would just need a little patience.

Laura lowered her legs and stretched, blissfully refreshed. But what time was it? She walked to the window and drew the curtains.

Evening!

Had she really slept all day?

'Oh goodness,' she sighed. 'Whatever must he think of me?' She stood in her flimsy petticoat, shivering. It was April but still chilly. Where were her clothes?

Just then a quiet knock came at the door. She padded across the room to open it. Antonio stood there with Maria in his arms. She was wearing a smile from cheek to pink cheek, and Laura gasped in delight.

'Sleep well?' he asked her, as he lowered Maria into her arms.

'Wonderfully, but you should have woken me.' Laura hugged her little girl and found a pair of dark eyes going slowly over her. She realized she was only wearing her silk petticoat and that her hair, if it had looked wild this morning, hadn't had a brush through it all day. 'I haven't dressed,' she apologized, embarrassed.

'There's no rush,' he said, his voice low and husky as his eyes dragged up to her face.

'Has she slept all afternoon?'

'A good part of it. Her temperature has dropped a little. It's still not back to normal, but she's happy enough, aren't you, titch?'

He grinned at Maria as she wriggled in Laura's arms. 'You found a T-shirt for her, too,' Laura said in surprise.

He smiled and his eyes seemed to be even darker. 'Indeed—and socks. Only we seem to have lost them somewhere. Maybe in her chair. I was just about to give her supper.'

'Supper? Good grief!' Laura flustered. 'But can you manage?' she asked doubtfully, wondering if he'd found the strained broth that Maria loved. 'Well, I'm sure you can,' she corrected herself, 'but don't you want to go home? Surely you must?'

'I'm in no hurry.' He shrugged, his broad shoulders lifting under his shirt. 'I busied myself with a little culinary activity.' He grinned. 'You'll forgive me for investigating your cupboards, but I've thrown a few things together. I was about to bring you a cup of tea, but I thought I heard noises. Shall I take her? Then you can shower and dress.'

He held out his hands and Laura placed Maria back in them. She went without a word, blowing more bubbles as he adjusted her in his arms. 'See you soon,' he said, and Maria gurgled over his shoulder as he bore her off to the kitchen.

Laura closed the door and leaned against it for a moment.

He had allowed her to sleep all afternoon and was now feeding Maria as though he did it every day of the week. It was a little too awe-inspiring to take in. He wasn't a married man so he couldn't have that much experience of babies, could he? But he seemed to be taking Maria in his stride. And hadn't he said something about throwing a few things together?

She still found it hard to believe as she showered and washed her hair and felt gloriously fresh afterwards. Choosing a soft pale green linen ankle-length dress to wear and towel-drying her hair, she decided to brush on lipstick and mascara.

Not because she wanted to look special for anyone in particular. But because all the worry of the past week had floated away. Or that was what she told herself as she looked in the mirror.

She liked this dress. It was summery and soft and a shade paler than her eyes. And being as tall as she was, she suited long frocks and skirts and trousers. Long legs had some advantage, she thought ruefully, even though they didn't always fit comfortably in small spaces.

Her hair was already drying as she left the bedroom. Her thick, tawny brown waves fell over her shoulders, glossy from the shampoo and conditioner and smelling of coconut. She knew it was useless to try to rearrange it, or even put it up immediately after washing. But she supposed it didn't matter. Antonio probably wouldn't notice anyway.

When she entered the kitchen, he was perched on one of Aunt M.'s breakfast barstools. His long legs stretched either side of the high chair, two moccasined feet planted squarely on the floor. He had a spoon in his hand and was gliding it around, making a whistle through his pursed lips. Maria was chuckling softly, her tiny mouth opening in anticipation as the spoon came close.

A floorboard creaked beneath Laura's feet. Two pair of eyes turned to look at her.

'Hi, there,' he called, and Maria squealed, banging her

palms together. He laughed softly. 'Yes, Mummy does look better, doesn't she?'

Laura felt colour flood into her cheeks as he gazed at her. 'Has she eaten all that?' she asked quickly, trying to ignore her racing pulse.

'Every last strained prune.' Maria slapped her tiny lips and wriggled to be free. He placed the bowl on the table and lifted her into his arms, dabbing her mouth with her bib. She blew bubbles and gave a little squeal. 'Thank you.' He laughed softly, handing her to Laura. 'I'll take that as a compliment.'

'Oh, I'm so pleased to see you looking better, darling,' Laura sighed, inhaling Maria's baby scent.

'The spots are out—everywhere,' he told her as he clattered dishes into the sink. 'A good sign. They'll hang around for a week or so. But the worst is over.'

Laura noted the lacy rash on her daughter's arms and legs. The rose-red spots seemed far less unpleasant now she knew what they were. She hugged Maria tightly. 'Thank you so much for all you've done,' she told him gratefully.

'I've enjoyed every moment.' Antonio was lathering the dishes, using generous squirts of soap. 'And I haven't quite finished. As I said, I put a little something on to cook for both of us. I hope you don't mind.'

'Mind?' Laura repeated, her eyes going to the range. 'Of course I don't mind. But don't you have something else to do?'

'Nothing as important as dining with two beautiful ladies.'

Laura thought he was joking, but he turned and studied her, his eyes going slowly over her hair and her dress. She felt embarrassed and she turned away, helping to clear the table with her free hand.

'What is it you're cooking?' she asked, trying to sound as though she hadn't heard what he'd just said.

'Pasta—there was some in the cupboard. A little cheese

sauce and salad. There were onions and tomatoes and some olive oil in the cupboard. And I put a little bread in the oven to warm.'

'I totally neglected food this week,' she said guiltily. 'You make it sound like a feast.'

He nodded, turning back to the sink. 'I hope so. *Mamma* taught us to make the most of every meal. To savour it— whatever it was. She loved to cook and I take after her more than any of my brothers.'

She walked slowly across the kitchen and sat on the stool, bouncing Maria on her knee. 'Have you a big family?'

'Four brothers,' he told her, and she gasped.

'Four!'

'I'm the youngest,' he told her, chuckling. Turning round, he pulled a face. 'And, so *Mamma* tells me, the most trouble.'

Laura found herself laughing. 'I don't believe it.'

'Oh, it's true,' he said seriously, giving her a dazzling smile to eclipse all smiles. He thrust out his chin and his eyes darkened like night as he made a dramatic face. 'I was always the one in trouble at school. Always the one who made Papa tear out his hair. And when I said I wanted to be a doctor, he told me he'd expect it of any of my brothers, but not me. He said I would be *un pesce fuor d'acqua*—a fish out of water! That I would be better suited to a kitchen.'

'But you obviously proved him wrong,' Laura prompted.

He nodded slowly as a soft sigh escaped his lips. 'Unfortunately, he never lived to see me finish my studies. He was a surgeon and worked too hard. Too hard and long for his heart. One day it just stopped—as he knew it would.'

'I'm so sorry,' Laura said quietly.

'You know what it's like to lose someone special,' he said, and she nodded, thinking of her parents and of Aunt M., too. And, of course, there was Mark. Though she hadn't really lost him, not in that way.

She hugged Maria tightly, the fears for her daughter filtering through her mind again. They came back when she wasn't on her guard and she stood up quickly and walked to the cooking range. It was old and expansively black and had been Aunt M.'s pride and joy.

'It looks delicious,' Laura said, as she noted all the ingredients were placed in their saucepans, ready to cook.

'Where do you usually eat?'

'In here.' She hesitated. 'We could use the dining room. Nothing's laid up, but I could sit Maria in her play-pen.'

Which was what she did, amazed at herself for suggesting such a thing because the dining room hadn't been used in ages and was probably damp and cold. She went half-heartedly along to the front of the guest-house. The dining room overlooked the sea and Laura hadn't gone in there in the last few weeks. It had been a beautiful room in its time and you could look out over the harbour and see from one end of the bay to the other.

But when she'd had Maria and had come to stay at Sea Breeze, it only made her recall the happy times when the guests had been here and the house had been buzzing with activity. So she'd locked the door and had started redecorating the other rooms.

As it was, the sun had warmed the big, high-ceilinged room. And when she opened the door, the half-drawn blinds let in a little of the evening dusk and the room really didn't look too bad. Just empty and alone. So she quickly drew the blinds so that she could see all the lights outside, twinkling along the promenade. Then she whisked off the white covers on the eight little tables and stacked them behind the mini-bar.

She chose one table by the window, then brought in Maria's play-pen. In just a few minutes she'd found a pristine white tablecloth and had spread Aunt M.'s silver on it. The little table lamps were all stacked neatly in a cupboard and Laura took out one, dusted its shade and set it in the middle of the table. The bulb still worked when she switched it on and it spread a creamy glow.

Maria was playing in her cot when she went in to fetch her. Dressing her in a warm towelling suit and gathering a few of her favourite toys, she took her into the dining room.

Antonio was there, two large plates of steaming food in his hand. On the table was a basket of hot bread and sliced butter, and in a little vase a single yellow primrose.

'From the kitchen garden.' He grinned as she walked towards him. 'Along with the basil.'

'That's beautiful,' she said, her breath taken away.

'I hope you'll say the same about supper,' he teased, setting the plates down.

Laura was still standing there, in shock at the transformation of the room she had almost been frightened of going into. She couldn't tell him that. She hadn't even wanted to admit it to herself. But there were ghosts in here now.

She lowered Maria into the play-pen she'd retrieved from the other room and sat her on a blanket, surrounded by her toys. She was soon occupied and Laura took her seat at the table.

He sat down in the chair opposite, then clicked his tongue. 'I forgot. The wine.'

'I haven't any,' she said as he rose and went to the door and disappeared for a few moments. He was back immediately with a bottle of red wine and two glasses.

'Where did you find that?' she asked in amazement.

He chuckled. 'In the boot of my car. One of my patients gave it to me last week.'

Which made Laura wonder who it had been, of course. Could it be the young woman she'd seen sitting with him? Laura waited for him to elaborate. But he didn't. Instead, he uncorked the bottle and poured them a glass each. But Laura didn't really need the wine. She was in heaven already.

CHAPTER FOUR

THE pasta was a masterpiece and so was the salad. Cobbled together from the few ingredients she'd had, he'd produced a feast. He'd even managed to make something of the ice cream, topping the simple vanilla with a sumptuous chocolate sauce.

'I can't believe you found all this in my cupboards.' Laura sat back in her seat and gazed at the empty dish. 'Your *mamma* taught you well.'

'Oh, yes, she did.' He nodded and took a sip of his wine. 'With five boys to cater for, and endless grandchildren, she's an expert.' A little smile trickled over his lips, and Laura wondered again why he'd never married. Becky had told her he was thirty-four, so he must have had many lovers by now.

But no way was she going to read anything more into what had happened between them. After all, he'd told her that it had been because she expected nothing from him that he'd offered help.

She was certain that's what he'd said, despite being half-asleep at the time. And he'd not given her any reason to think otherwise. To use Becky's least favourite word, he'd just been kind.

'More wine?' he asked, lifting the bottle, but she shook her head. Neither of them had finished the first glass. Whilst pregnant and breastfeeding Maria, she hadn't touched a drop. And even now that Maria was bottle-fed and her own body had got back into shape, wine still wasn't tempting.

In all honesty it was probably because she didn't want to relax completely. If she did, the chances were her mind would wander to Mark. She didn't want anything to penetrate her defences—she was doing fine. Perfectly fine. And that was the way she was going to keep her life. Even. Uncomplicated. Selfishly full of Maria and of no one else.

Besides, wine was a luxury. And at the moment she couldn't afford those extra pennies. And the meal tonight, despite its simple ingredients, had been luxury enough.

Laura studied Antonio's strong, classical features in the light of the table lamp. How stunning his dark eyes were. So Latin, so seductive. On their surface, she could see herself reflected, the pale green of her dress, her face hidden in shadow. All she could see clearly was a tumble of waves spilling over her shoulders and the light catching the tops of her arms.

But underneath her reflection his eyes were a breathtaking burnt umber, the colour of earth when restored by rain. When he moved slightly, they glimmered and grew even brighter, or was it darker, obviously an illusion? She couldn't fathom it out. But, whatever they did, they were magnetic and she had to drag her attention back to the present.

'Coffee?' he said then, an eyebrow tugging up.

'Mmm. That would be lovely.'

'In here?' he asked, casting a glance at Maria. 'Or do you want to take Maria somewhere a little warmer?'

There was, Laura realized, just the kitchen or the small room next door to it. The kitchen was warm from the range, but the fire in the sitting room hadn't been lit for weeks.

'There's one little sitting room,' Laura murmured. 'But it's probably freezing in there.'

'Is that the room next to the kitchen?'

She nodded.

'I lit a fire in there,' he told her with a grin. 'I thought you might need it. There was enough coal in the shed. And a few logs. It's banked down now, but I think you'll find it cosy enough.'

She stared at Antonio in wonder. 'I don't believe this.'

He frowned. 'You don't believe what?'

'Just—*everything*,' she said breathlessly. 'I mean, you come to help me in your own time. You stay all day whilst I sleep. You care for my daughter and feed her and cook a meal, too. And then this…making up a fire…'

'Thank my *mamma*.' He laughed softly, his deep chuckle reminding her of the smooth, rich sauce he'd made for the ice cream. 'Messing about in the kitchen is a great leveller. And eating a meal in such pleasant company made me forget about work.'

'But you weren't *supposed* to be at work,' Laura reminded him firmly. 'You would have gone home if I hadn't phoned and, well, done whatever it was you had planned for Good Friday.'

'I'd have worked.' He shrugged. 'You see, the books I was retrieving from my desk are medical tomes. I'm researching and writing a series of articles for a medical journal.'

Laura's green eyes widened. 'What subject?'

'Hands, would you believe? Subheading—''Our Key Diagnostic Tool''.'

'Fascinating,' Laura said, a little surprised.

'We tend to take them for granted. In Europe and the States, the anatomy and purpose of the hands is given more attention than here. I'm hoping to remedy the situation a little.' He grinned, leaning his head to one side. 'But don't get me started.'

'Why not? I'm interested.'

His smile seemed to last for ever. 'You're sweet, Laura. Very sweet.' He was looking at her with that strange expression again, half curious, half abstracted, and suddenly she realized that neither of them were moving. His eyes met hers again and she found herself wondering what he was thinking and where exactly they were going with their relationship.

Then suddenly he averted his gaze and pushed back his chair. 'Go in by the fire with Maria,' he told her in a rather clipped voice. 'I'll bring you coffee.'

She looked up at him. 'What about you?'

For a moment she thought he was about to say that he'd join her, but then he shook his head. 'It's time I went.'

'But—it doesn't seem fair,' she flustered. 'I mean, you've done all the hard work. At least have some coffee.'

But he shook his head again. 'The meal was sufficient— thank you.'

She felt as though she had walked under a cold shower. She had thought he was going to make coffee for them both. She'd pictured them in the little room, all cosy and snug, with the embers of the fire still burning in the grate as they sat in front of it.

She'd even heard their voices. She asking him about his family, his brothers, and how he'd come to settle in England. And he telling her, sitting so close on the tiny sofa that their arms touched, his shirt smooth against her skin like silk.

'Are you certain?' she asked again.

'Positive. Off you both go.' He began to clear the dishes.

Laura felt somehow in the way, as if he really didn't want her to help. So she picked up Maria and went along to the sitting room. It was filled with the golden light of the coals as the fire smouldered in the grate. There was a smoky scent clinging to the air and it made her think more of autumn rather than spring. She sat on the sofa and hugged Maria. The place seemed so homely. Like it used to be when Aunt M. was alive.

Dangerous, she thought helplessly. Very dangerous.

I don't want Antonio to go.

I don't want him to leave.

I want tonight to go on for ever. She closed her eyes and laid her cheek thoughtfully against Maria's head. Had she said or done something to offend him? But, no, that was silly. She was imagining things. The sooner she got back to reality the better.

Antonio brought her coffee, said that he was sure Maria

would be brighter in the morning, ran a gentle hand over her tiny head—and left.

Afterwards, Laura managed to block out her silly notions. She played with Maria until her eyes were closing. She was asleep even before Laura put her in her cot.

The fire was too much of a luxury to leave, so Laura brought in her duvet and slept that night on the sofa. She left the door open so she could hear Maria, but she didn't wake until six the next morning.

The kitchen had been thoroughly cleared the night before. As Laura prepared breakfast, the neat piles of stacked dishes and spotless worktop made her think of yesterday. She hauled her mind back, promising herself she wasn't going to have a repeat performance of the blues.

But when she went into the sitting room and saw the embers in the grate, she swallowed and cleared her throat. Had yesterday really happened?

And why had Antonio suddenly disappeared? His attitude had been puzzling. Not cool. Not brusque. But oddly formal. Or had she imagined it?

Laura fled from the room and took Maria into the garden. It was wonderfully warm and spring-like. The chill in the air had vanished and Maria, well protected against the sun, sat in her buggy, happy to watch Laura pottering about.

Not that Laura did much. Everywhere she looked she saw him, which had been why she had come out in the first place.

To forget him.

The primrose, the basil, the coal. Everything reminded her. Even Maria's little shrieks of delight.

'You're behaving like an adolescent,' Laura scolded herself, but she soon admitted defeat and wheeled the buggy back indoors. At bathtime, Maria's spots were happily gathered on her arms and legs, but the rash on her cheeks had disappeared. And by Sunday morning, they were healthily pink again.

'We'll go to the harbour,' Laura decided, and threw on

shorts and a T-shirt and pulled out the sun canopy on the buggy.

It was a delicious Easter Sunday, full of warm April promise. Maria wore her sun hat and denim dungarees and Laura felt exhilarated as she walked down the hill. The breeze rippled through her hair and the smell of the sea was intoxicating.

A dozen or so boats were moored in the harbour, bobbing up and down on the tide. Laura headed for the little café opposite.

'Hello, sweetheart,' the owner said to Maria as Laura pushed the buggy next to one of the outside tables. 'Have you had your Easter egg yet?'

Laura laughed softly. 'No, but we're about to make up for it, Molly. Could we have some of your delicious chocolate cake?'

'Coming up right away.' Molly grinned, giving Maria a wink.

Laura lazed back on her white plastic seat in the shade of the big umbrella. Aunt M. had known the couple who owned the café, but now Molly and her husband ran it as more of a bistro.

Molly brought out the goodies and Maria gave a little squeal as she saw the cake. Laura fed her some, and between them both it soon disappeared.

'I see I've arrived too late,' a deep voice said, and Laura looked up, quickly dabbing her mouth.

'Dr…I mean…' she spluttered, 'Antonio!' She blinked as the tall shadow fell across her.

'I thought I might find you here.'

'Did you? There's nothing wrong is there?'

He laughed. 'Nothing at all.' He wore sunglasses, so she couldn't see his eyes, but he had a wonderful smile and her heart banged against her ribs. His skin looked like copper in a light blue T-shirt and shorts that revealed long, powerful legs that ended in soft leather thongs. 'I called at Sea Breeze and when there was no reply I wondered if you'd strolled down to the harbour.' He caught sight of Maria under her canopy and bent down. 'Hello, little one.'

She gave him a smile that said it all, locking her little fingers around his hand. 'She's better?' he asked Laura.

'Oh, much.'

'And the rash has gone?'

'On her cheeks, yes.'

He nodded slowly, chuckling as Maria offered him one of her toys. After a while he stood up and drew out a chair. 'May I?'

Laura shrugged. 'Of course.'

'You're not expecting anyone?'

'No. It was just nice to get out of the house.'

'Have you had any thoughts about the crèche next week?' he asked, sitting down beside her.

She'd had plenty but had arrived at no decision. She couldn't send Maria to crèche with spots and, even though she had Easter Monday off, it wasn't likely they would have cleared by Tuesday.

'I know the infection isn't contagious now…' She hesitated. 'And the crèche would probably take her, but I don't know how I feel about leaving her.' She shrugged, tailing off. 'At the same time, I don't want to let you down either.'

He nodded thoughtfully. 'Which is why I wanted to see you,' he said quietly, and her heart sank. He slid off his sunglasses and tucked them slowly in his pocket. Laura swallowed as she looked into his eyes. Was he going to say that they needed someone more reliable at the centre?

Laura held her breath as Maria gave a squeal. Antonio smiled down at her, returning the fluffy bear he held in his hands. 'But first,' he said, as though to Maria, 'I came to wish you both a happy Easter and…' He paused and Laura waited again. 'And to apologize for leaving so abruptly on Friday night.' He turned slowly to look at her. 'It was the er…*article*…you understand?'

'Did you manage to write anything when you got home?'

A grin spread across his face. 'No. As a matter of fact, I didn't.'

'Oh, dear,' Laura sighed. 'I'm sorry. I feel responsible.'

'And I feel slightly ridiculous,' he admitted with a shrug. 'My leaving achieved nothing but a deep regret I hadn't been able to share your fire.'

Laura didn't know what to say. Did he really mean he had wanted to stay or was he just saying that so she didn't feel guilty?

'And now for the other matter,' he continued more seriously as a frown furrowed his forehead. Laura was suddenly convinced she was right. He had been pleasant in order to soften the blow of firing her.

But just as he spoke there was an ear-piercing scream and they looked across the road to the harbour. Laura saw a young woman standing on the deck of one of the boats. She was waving her arms and pointing to the water.

Suddenly everyone was running and Molly came out of the café, along with all her customers. Antonio wasted no time in pushing back his chair and running across the road, and Laura saw him disappear into the crowd.

'What's happened?' Molly asked anxiously.

'I don't know.' Laura stepped out of the shade of the umbrella and shielded her eyes from the sun. 'I think someone's fallen in.'

Molly groaned. 'It's high tide, too. The current is really dangerous between the boats.'

'Molly, would you stay with Maria?' Laura asked hurriedly. 'I might be able to help Antonio if there's a casualty.'

Molly took hold of the buggy. 'You go, love. I'll wheel her inside. No one will be in whilst there's a panic on. Be careful, though. Don't go falling in yourself.'

Laura gave Maria's hand a squeeze and then ran across the road. The slipway was crammed with onlookers, but the woman was still screaming and Laura pushed her way through to the wall and the railing that ran along the edge of it.

'Someone fell overboard,' a man said beside her. 'And then this bloke jumped in. I hope he's a strong swimmer. He looks tough enough, but that's a heck of a current out there.'

Laura looked into the water and saw Antonio. She watched in horror as he powered toward the boat, his body gliding through the water like a fish. Then suddenly he seemed to stop as he neared the boat and disappeared under the surface.

'That's where the man fell in,' another voice said. 'I saw it happen. The girl threw in one of those lifebelts. But the man didn't seem to be able to hold it.'

Laura felt sick as she gazed at the spot she'd last seen Antonio. There was nothing there or by the boat, just the lifebelt drifting away. It must have only been seconds but it felt like a lifetime before she saw him again. He came up with a gasp, his sleek brown body surfacing with a splash. She watched as he looked around, treading the water and slapping back his hair from his eyes.

'He hasn't found him,' the man said. 'Look, he's going down again!'

Laura watched breathlessly as Antonio turned upside down so that his feet were the last thing visible as he disappeared below the surface. A hush descended and even the woman on the boat was quiet, her hands held up to her face.

Then suddenly two heads bobbed up and there was an audible sigh of relief from the crowd. 'He's got him,' the man said. 'And he's bringing him back to the wall.'

Laura pushed her way through the crowd to the harbour steps. Two men were already there, arms outstretched.

'Has someone called an ambulance?' Laura shouted, and one of the men turned to look at her.

'My wife has,' he replied. 'She ran over to the gift shop to phone. It shouldn't be long.'

A few seconds later Antonio reached the steps and supported the man until they were able to grasp him and pull him up. He was unconscious and Laura reached out to help as they carried him up.

Antonio hauled his lean, muscled body from the sea and took the steps in two leaps. They laid the man down and Antonio knelt beside him, shaking the water from his face. Laura knelt beside him. 'Is there a pulse?'

Antonio felt. 'No. You do recognize him, don't you?'

Laura looked down at the man's face. 'Mitchell Fraser!' she said in astonishment.

Antonio nodded, then shouted to the crowd, 'Can someone get a boat over to the woman?'

Someone said they'd see to it and Antonio gave her a grim little smile. 'We'll start CPR and respiration, OK?' She nodded as he tore open Mitchell Fraser's soaked shirt and began artificial respiration and chest compressions. After a while Laura continued, keeping the same even rhythm, but there was no response and she was beginning to think that it was useless.

'One last try. I'll take over the compressions, you take a rest,' Antonio said, and she sat back on her heels breathlessly, her arms aching from the effort. She watched him work tirelessly, as though he refused to be beaten, but she knew the minutes were ticking away.

Then suddenly a tremor went through the body.

'We've got him,' Antonio shouted as Mitchell convulsed and threw up. 'He swallowed half the harbour by the looks of it.'

Laura helped Antonio push Mitchell into the recovery position and a woman brought rugs from her car. A man donated his jacket.

Antonio thanked them, glancing at Laura. 'That water was freezing. The danger now is hypothermia.'

Luckily the ambulance arrived and by the time they wrapped him up and the paramedics were there, Mitchell was fully conscious.

'Will you go with him?' Laura asked as they lifted him on board.

Antonio nodded. 'His pulse is slow and his respirations are weak. I'm a bit worried about his pupillary and tendon reflexes. They don't seem to be there. But once we insulate him and get him into Intensive Care, we'll stand a better chance of seeing what the damage is.' He squeezed Laura's arm. 'You were terrific. Thanks.'

She smiled. 'You'd better get warm.'

'I'm OK.' He grinned, but she saw that water still rippled down his body. His shorts were soaked, clinging to his hips and muscled thighs. His bronzed body looked lean and athletic and Laura knew that only a superbly fit physique could have achieved such a rescue. 'I'll phone you,' he told her as he jumped up into the ambulance.

Laura nodded, standing back as the doors closed and the siren wailed out. She watched the vehicle carefully negotiate the harbour wall, then disappear up the hill.

Back in the café Molly was sitting at one of the tables, with Maria on her lap. Laura thanked her and took Maria. Molly glanced through the window to the quay. 'What happened? Is he all right? It was a man, wasn't it?'

Laura nodded. 'It was a close call, but he's conscious at least.'

'How did he fall in?'

'I've no idea.'

'Your friend managed to revive him?'

'Yes,' Laura agreed. 'Luckily.'

'He's a strong swimmer to have got him back to the wall, you know. Must be a very fit man. Not many people could have done what he did.'

Laura sighed. 'I just hope the man wasn't under too long.'

'Only that woman will know, I suppose,' Molly observed, standing up to look out of the window. 'Look, she's just coming up the steps. Someone's brought her over by boat. She looks dreadful.'

Laura stood up and watched the little group on the quay-side. The woman was still crying and someone put a jacket round her shoulders. Molly touched Laura's arm. 'I'll just go and see if she wants a cup of tea. I expect she's in shock.'

'That's a good idea,' Laura agreed. 'Then she really should go to the hospital and give what information she can.'

Molly gave her a nod. 'I'll suggest it. Your little girl was a gem, by the way.' She smiled down at Maria. 'Not a peep out of her. Oh, someone brought in a T-shirt and thongs and a set of car keys.' She went behind the counter and brought over a carrier bag. 'I expect they belong to your friend. Do you want to take them?'

Laura looked inside and recognized the T-shirt and thongs, but she wasn't certain about the keys. They were probably Antonio's, and if they weren't she could always hand them in at the police station tomorrow. 'Put them on the buggy, Molly, would you? I'll give them to him.'

After Molly had gone, Laura left the café and wondered who the girl was that had been with Mitchell Fraser. A relative? A friend?

Maria gave an impatient squeal and Laura set off up the hill, her legs feeling wobbly after all the excitement. The accident had been a close call and she shivered, thinking of Mitchell Fraser and his close encounter with death. But as she turned into the narrow road of terraced guest-houses, she saw Antonio's four-wheel-drive parked there and her thoughts flew to him.

He must have left it there to walk down the hill to the harbour. Laura felt a warm wave of anticipation run through her. She'd see him again today when he came to collect it. And then she could return his things. She'd also find out what he had been about to tell her before the accident had happened.

But did she really want to know? she wondered as she pushed Maria inside. But her mind wouldn't co-operate with common sense. She tried not to remember what he'd looked like this afternoon as he'd bent over Mitchell Fraser. Even under those frightening circumstances, she'd been wholly aware of the power of Antonio's presence. His strength, his maleness and his utter determination to fight for the man's life. How in heaven's name could she be objective?

But she had to be. On Friday she'd come seriously close to lowering her defences. What if she had? Would he have taken advantage of the situation? No, she couldn't put their relationship to the test.

Trust was something she would have to re-learn. Maybe one day she would. Or maybe not. But if her affair with Mark had taught her anything, it was that she could never expose herself to such pain again.

It was a lesson she had no intention of repeating, especially with a man like Antonio Dallori.

Laura glanced out of the dining room window at seven-thirty that evening. Antonio's four-wheel-drive was still there and there'd been no telephone call. She was trying not to open the plastic bag Molly had given her.

But some tortured instinct made her take out the T-shirt, lay it against her cheek and inhale his aroma. She knew as she breathed the lemony tang into her lungs that she was crazy. Out of her mind. What was she doing? And as if that wasn't enough, she lifted the thongs and drew her fingers over the supple, sexy Italian leather. She knew they were Italian—they couldn't be anything else.

They had fitted his feet so perfectly. Well-shaped feet that were dusky and strong and perfectly boned. Feet could be ignored in many people, but not his. They were firm, masculine feet that had marvellous arches and well-groomed toes.

Laura was ashamed of herself. She felt like a voyeur. So she put his things back quickly and left them in the hall.

What to do now? she wondered restlessly. Maria was fast

asleep so she had better make the most of her time. There was plenty to do. First on the list was the bedroom on the first floor. It needed a lick of paint before the agents showed anyone else round. It was the small things that had probably put people off before. Well, she'd transformed the private quarters with minimal expense—no reason not to start on the first floor.

The wallpaper in the room was good. But the door and window-frame needed freshening. And a horrendous stain had ruined the carpet. So it was a question of taking the carpet up or covering it. Probably it would be less expensive to do the latter.

She was upstairs, considering the stain, her brow knitted in a frown of indecision, when the doorbell went. Her heart jumped crazily and she flew downstairs. When she got to the front door, she knew it was Antonio. His tall frame waited outside the Victorian glass panel.

When she opened it, he smiled, but her heart clenched because he looked so tired. He was wearing his shorts and a white T-shirt and a pair of boating shoes, neither of which she recognized.

'Lost property at the hospital,' he told her, following her gaze. 'Sorry it's so late.'

'Have you eaten?' she asked as he stepped in and she closed the door. He looked lean and hungry but he shook his head and stood where he was.

'I don't want anything, thanks,' he said, and mustered up a grin. 'I need to shower first.'

'Are you all right?' she asked anxiously.

He nodded, his dark eyes heavy, their long lashes beating slowly down on his cheeks. There were little crinkles of weariness at their corners and his cheeks looked hollow, but, then, they have every right to be, Laura thought as she gazed at him.

'Is Maria asleep?'

She nodded. 'Yes. Can't I offer you a drink—or something stronger?'

'No. I'm driving and, anyway, I need to eat first.'

'How's Mitchell Fraser?' she asked, and he heaved a sigh.

'Fifty-fifty at the moment. The woman, who says she's his girlfriend, came to the hospital. She said they'd been sleeping on the boat and partying the night before. Today, apparently, he continued drinking and, according to her, simply missed his footing on the deck.'

'And the prognosis?' she asked uncertainly.

'Not good, really. He has hypotension and hypothermia, as well as hypoxia and acidosis.'

'Isn't acidosis associated with diabetes mellitus?' Laura asked with a frown.

'Yes, but in gaseous acidosis more than the normal amount of carbon dioxide is retained in the body. In other words, he's quite unstable. They'll have to monitor him closely and watch for a drop in arterial blood pressure.'

'The next few hours will be crucial,' Laura said. 'Poor man.'

'His BP was unpleasantly low when we got him there.' He shrugged, thrusting back his hair with a slow hand. 'One of the casualty staff was going off duty and offered me a lift. There was nothing I could do so I came here.'

Laura looked up at him. 'You must be exhausted.'

'Not really. Just…' Antonio lifted his broad shoulders '…frustrated that I couldn't talk some sense into him the day he came to see me.'

'He wasn't ready to listen,' Laura said softly. 'Maybe something like this will change his life.'

He drew his lips into a tight line. 'Maybe. If he recovers.'

They were silent for a moment then she reached for the carrier bag. 'Molly, at the café, gave me this. Your T-shirt and thongs. And there's some keys in there, too. I didn't try them in your car. Are they yours?'

'Yes,' he said with a relieved smile, and took them. 'I must have thrown them out of my pocket before I dived in—a kind of reflex action. I was wondering how I was going to drive home.' His smile faded as he added hesitantly, 'I'm sorry we didn't have much time to talk. There was something I was about to say…' She waited, preparing herself for the worst. 'We were discussing Maria, and the crèche…'

She nodded and he paused as his dark eyes flickered slowly over her. 'The thing is, my mother is arriving from Italy tomorrow,' he said, arching an eyebrow. 'She's on holiday with me for a month or so. And, well…please, don't feel you have to go along with this, but I'm quite sure she would have Maria for you.' He gave a little shrug, frowning at her doubtfully. 'As I said, please, don't feel you have to accept. The other alternative is that you take the week off. I'm quite certain Becky can cope.'

Laura stared at him wordlessly. It was the last thing on earth she'd expected him to say. 'But what would your mother think? I mean, she's here on holiday. Not to look after a baby.'

'As I told you, she lives for her grandchildren. She adores babies. It would give her great pleasure—and fill what might have been a few lonely hours.'

Laura shook her head. 'I'm sure you're just saying that.'

'Why would I?' he asked reasonably. 'If you would entrust Maria to her, and Maria is content to stay, I think the arrangement would serve all our purposes.'

Laura gave a little sigh. 'I don't think I could.'

'But why?' he asked, his frown deepening. 'Is it Maria?'

'No… She does seem better tonight…'

'Would you prefer to take time off?'

'No, not at all. But—'

'Then the matter is settled.' Antonio smiled softly, his eyes so deep and dark that she couldn't tear them away. 'Ring me tomorrow and we'll make arrangements. You have my home telephone number?'

She nodded. 'Yes, I've got the phone list.'

'Good.' He paused as he opened the door. 'Thank you for all you did today.'

She shrugged. 'It was nothing.'

He began to say something, then pulled back his shoulders and left. She watched him climb into his vehicle, pulling his long, muscular legs inside and pulling the door to. The window buzzed down and he looked at her as he started the engine. Their eyes met for a moment, until he gave a brief nod and drove off.

Laura went back in and stood in the hall, gazing out over the dusky pink horizon. Was she dreaming all this? Or was it really happening?

She didn't know. She was far too confused to try to fathom any of it at the moment. Certainly not Antonio's motives in all this. Or her own, which she had given up trying to define as her heart leapt, way out of control, inside her chest.

CHAPTER FIVE

'WOULD it be possible,' Antonio said, 'for you to call this afternoon? Then you can see where I live. And you'll have a better idea of who you'll be leaving Maria with tomorrow. Of course, if you haven't time…' He left the sentence unfinished and Laura bit her lip, trying to fathom out why she felt so uneasy about the offer.

It was unexpected, yes. But what had Antonio told his mother? And why, anyway, would an elderly lady welcome the responsibility of a stranger's child?

'Antonio…' she began, but stopped as she searched for the words she really wanted to say.

'You would prefer to take the week off?' he suggested impassively.

'No—it's just that I don't want to burden your mother.'

'Burden?' A short chuckle came over the line. 'I think not. Quite the reverse.'

Laura gazed out of the window, wishing that she'd simply agreed to take the week off. After all, he'd suggested it. And she could always make up the time. Instead, she'd got herself into this position and it seemed ungrateful not to accept.

'What time shall I come?' she said eventually. If Signora Dallori took an instant dislike to her, then so be it. And it would solve all the problems if she did.

'It's midday now…so about three?' Antonio suggested. 'You know where I live?'

'Your address is on Maggie's list, isn't it?'

'Drive past the centre,' he answered, 'take the third on the left at the next roundabout. That will bring you out of

75

the town and onto the cliff. You'll come to a lane—turn down it. Canzone del Mare is just a short way along.'

What if Antonio's mother was frail? Or tired from her journey? Laura wondered after she rang off. And what, in heaven's name, was she going to say to her?

The next problem was finding something to wear. Several skirts, a sundress and a pair of cotton trousers later she still hadn't decided.

'Well, *you* look perfect, darling,' Laura sighed as she lowered Maria onto the floor beside her toys. She looked cute in her baggy pink shorts and sun hat. 'But Mummy can't make up her mind.'

Laura was tempted to wear shorts and a top, too. It was a beautiful day, not a cloud in the sky. If they'd been staying at home, she would simply have relaxed in old stuff.

Laura sighed impatiently. For heaven's sake, she was just paying someone a call, not going for an interview! But she didn't want to look like something dragged in from the rain. So she rummaged in her wardrobe again, regretting that she'd left most of her things in the London flat. Her friend had brought down a suitcase full after Maria's birth, but most of them were winter clothes.

Then she caught sight of the dress Shelley had given her.

'Keep it for when you lose your bump,' Shelley had joked. 'This little number is wicked. Miles too small for me. You're welcome to it.'

Laura hadn't tried it on then. A week after Maria's birth, she hadn't thought it would fit either. But it might now.

The frock was a soft, summery pale green, calf-length and belted at the waist. Black strappy heels would go with it, she decided as she tried it on, scooping up her hair into a clip. The dress fitted—Shelley had been right. The tiny waist emphasized her height and long legs. If she'd gained any excess weight whilst pregnant it had all disappeared now.

'Hmm,' she pondered in the mirror. 'What do you think, Maria?'

Maria gurgled.

Laura laughed. 'So I pass the test?' Kissing her daughter lightly, Laura slipped on shoes and decided to quit whilst she was ahead.

At half past two, she drove into Charbourne, following directions to the Old Coast Road. She hadn't come this way in years and only just remembered the lane that snaked off to the left.

What she had no recollection of was the new development that had been built along it. Canzone del Mare stood out from the other houses, all pretty and unique in their own way. But the villa was something else. Its white stucco walls gleamed in the sunshine, as did the shuttered windows with their half-moon arches. The roof was flat and cinnamon-tiled and a long sandy drive led up to the heavy oak front door.

Laura parked in the drive and lifted Maria from her seat. The door opened and a woman walked out to greet them. She was tall and slender, with black hair coiled up on her head. Her eyes were dark and piercing and she smiled warmly and held out her hand.

'Laura, isn't it? And this must be Maria.' Without a shred of shyness, Maria offered her fluffy bear and Signora Dallori took it. 'Thank you, Maria. Antonio has told me all about you.' She turned to Laura. 'My son won't be long. He had to visit a patient.' She spoke faultless English and Laura wondered why she had assumed Signora Dallori would be a frail, elderly woman. Perhaps because Antonio had mentioned she was a grandmother, which, of course, didn't automatically make her ancient!

'Please, come in,' she went on pleasantly, and led the way through the house. It was built in Mediterranean style, with simple stone walls, solid wooden furniture and smooth tiled floors. The drawing room was stylish, furnished in simple but chic elegance, and the wide glass windows were thrown open to the sea.

Laura walked onto the terrace and Charbourne Bay

spread out in front of her, a breathtaking panorama of sea and sky. 'How beautiful,' she sighed, stepping towards the balcony wall. Her eyes followed the curve of land to her right. 'I remember walking these cliffs with my aunt,' she murmured reflectively. 'But it was just grass and a sheer drop years ago. Since then all these houses have sprung up.'

'Canzone del Mare was built three years ago,' Signora Dallori explained. 'It means Song of the Sea. Antonio designed the house and had it built to his specifications, following the style of our family home in Capri.'

'Capri?' Laura repeated, intrigued.

'Yes, I was born on the island. Antonio's father and I lived there and also here in England. Antonio's grandfather was Italian but his grandmother was English. They lived in Surrey, where we also kept a home. Roberto, my husband, travelled a great deal. His work as a heart specialist took him all over the world.'

Laura nodded thoughtfully. 'Italy is such a beautiful country.'

'You've visited there?'

Laura nodded. 'Just for holidays.' She paused. 'Do you still have a home in Surrey?'

'No, my brother-in-law lives there, though. After my husband died, he offered to buy our house and I agreed and returned to Capri.' Signora Dallori shrugged. 'It seemed the best thing to do at the time. I missed my grandchildren.' She gestured to a long wooden table filled with food. 'Now, Laura, please, sit down. Will Maria sit on your lap? Or shall I hold her? Will she come to me?'

Laura laughed as Maria stretched out her plump little arms. 'I think she understood what you said.'

'She is so friendly,' Signora Dallori said, looking enchanted as she took Maria in her arms.

'Yes, I'm very lucky,' Laura admitted. 'She is a friendly little soul.'

Laura gazed at the table. There were pitchers of cool

drinks and bowls of bread and fruit, a gourmet-sized quiche and a bowl of tossed salad with onions, olives and tomatoes. Laura wondered a little guiltily if Signora Dallori had spent all morning preparing for her visit.

Just then a tall figure stepped through the glass doors. 'Antonio!' his mother said, with a smile. As soon as he appeared, Laura was aware of his presence. His straight black hair was combed back across his head, tapering down to the collar of his pale blue shirt. Laura thought how Mediterranean he looked, his olive skin darker now in the sunshine and his straight Roman nose making his mouth seem more sensual as he smiled, his white teeth glimmering under the soft, full lips.

Laura realized she was staring and was grateful when Maria squealed in recognition. Antonio went to her, hunkering down beside his mother, and Maria grasped his fingers.

'I didn't realise you were on call,' she said quickly, trying to tear her eyes away from the strong, tanned hands and their well-shaped nails. 'I wouldn't have come if I'd known.'

'Which is why I didn't mention it.' His eyes met hers and a thrill went through her as the hooded lids fell lazily over the deep, dark pupils. He seemed to have the most extraordinary effect on her and Laura looked quickly at Signora Dallori who, thank goodness, didn't appear to have noticed her reaction.

'Your mother has gone to so much trouble,' she said, her voice slightly shaky.

'Of course.' He shrugged nonchalantly. 'That's how we do it in Italy, isn't it, *Mamma*?'

Signora Dallori crooked an eyebrow. 'But I would be surprised, Laura, if Antonio has more than a cup of coffee when on his own. Now, Antonio, take Maria for me whilst I offer our guest something to eat.'

'*Mamma* still isn't convinced I can look after myself,' he commented teasingly, as he lifted Maria into his arms.

'Most men only think they can.' His mother smiled as she bent over the table and glanced at Laura. 'Isn't that so, Laura?'

Laura nodded, smiling, happy to be included in the easy rapport between mother and son. But she could only imagine what it must be like to enjoy the presence of a male figure in her life. It was what she had wanted for her own children, the make-believe family that she had always imagined she would create with the man of her dreams.

Instead, she had rushed into love, giving her trust to someone who had never intended to love her. And because of that, Maria had been cheated. And as she looked at Antonio standing at the balcony with her child in his arms, a voice inside her warned that no man could be trusted. Remember your mistakes, it urged her. Learn by them.

'Now, little one, what do you think of the sea?' he murmured in a voice that rippled like cream. And Laura's eyes lingered on his broad shoulders straining under the blue material, his arms locked protectively around her daughter. She felt her mouth go dry as Maria's laughter trickled back like a tiny tinkle of bells.

'Laura, now you must eat,' Signora Dallori said gently, and she accepted the plate of delicious food that was set before her. As she looked up into Antonio's mother's face, she wondered what she was thinking as her son spoke accomplished baby-talk without the faintest hint of self-consciousness.

Indeed, Laura was wondering herself, still feeling as though she were part of a dream in the seductively attractive atmosphere of Canzone del Mare.

It was an extraordinary afternoon. It was as if she had known the Dallori family for years, as they sat companionably on the terrace bathed in soft sunlight and talked away the hours. Then Antonio swept away the dishes and disappeared into the house, leaving Laura alone with his mother.

Signora Dallori spoke of her other sons, Marco, Luca, Pietro and Roberto, and Laura lost count of the grandchildren who made up the large and expanding numbers of the big Italian family.

'Now, you must tell me something about yourself, Laura,' she said, and Laura, realizing she had hardly contributed much about her own childhood, sketched in her life at Sea Breeze after her parents had died.

'Your aunt sounds a wonderful woman, Laura,' Antonio's mother commented.

'She was. And I still miss her.'

'Of course you must. She represented both mother and father for you.'

Laura felt her cheeks tingle with pride. 'Aunt M. gave me all the love and security I could have wanted. And she encouraged me when I said I wanted to train in London. I was young,' Laura said with a reflective smile, 'and it was the place to be. Once Aunt M. was confident that I had made up my mind, she did everything to help me.'

'So what does the future have in store for you?' Signora Dallori asked eventually, and Laura paused, thinking carefully before she replied.

'My plan is to move back to London and to the flat that I share with my friend Shelley,' she said after a while. 'But I have to sell Sea Breeze first, and with the equity I can look for a property closer to the City, or at least within easy commuting distance. Shelley and I might share a mortgage, which would give us a better choice in the property market.'

Signora Dallori nodded slowly. 'I assume that in the City you will have a greater choice of work? Or is it that you prefer to live there?'

'Charbourne is my home,' Laura replied, and glanced at her daughter who sat on a rug on the tiled floor, playing with her toys, 'but, as a single parent, I need to find a job that will enable me to support Maria and give us security.

I trained in London and worked there and have contacts that I'll use. At least, that's the idea so far.'

'You are very brave, Laura,' the older woman said without guile. 'And a very independent young woman. I respect that.'

Just then Maria gave a yawn and screwed up her face. 'I think we're probably outstaying our welcome.' Laura sighed gratefully as she rose and lifted Maria into her arms. 'Thank you so much for the wonderful meal, Signora Dallori.'

Laura realized it was almost six o'clock. She had been sitting on the terrace and enjoying the sunshine and company for more than three hours and she felt a little guilty for taking up so much of their time.

Signora Dallori helped her to gather her things and then walked with her to the door. 'I'm very happy to have Maria,' she assured Laura before she left. 'She is a delightful child.'

'But this *is* your holiday,' Laura pointed out, still hesitant. 'And a holiday is meant for relaxing.'

'And relax I shall. Maria will occupy my attention and the housework will remain ignored.'

Laura laughed softly. 'Yes, there is that upside to being with children.'

Signora Dallori laughed, too. 'Ah, here is Antonio. Goodbye until tomorrow, Laura. *Ciao, bambina,*' she murmured, and placed her hands on Maria's, squeezing them gently.

Antonio accompanied Laura to the car and waited as she fastened Maria into her seat, then climbed in herself.

'Thank you for such a pleasant afternoon,' she said as Antonio leaned down and looked in. 'Your mother is so welcoming. I wanted to offer to pay her but I don't think she would have liked me to. But I pay the crèche and it only seems right to…well, make some gesture…'

'No, she would not accept payment,' he told her, his dark eyes enveloping her as she looked up at him.

'But I can't just take and not give something in return.'

'You have already given.' His smile made her bones melt as his eyes locked with hers. 'Looking after Maria will provide *Mamma* with an interest. I'm away all day and she knows no one in this area. As I told you before, the arrangement is of benefit to us all.'

The sun was playing softly on his face and his dark eyes were the colour of coals, deep and impenetrable, and she wondered if what he had told her was really the truth.

'Are you on call for the rest of the evening?' she asked.

He nodded. 'My official duty was next weekend, but I'm taking *Mamma* to London so Jamie swapped with me. He was happy to have the Easter Monday with his family.'

'Well, I hope you don't have too many interruptions.' She smiled, her hand on the keys, but as she was about to start the car, she gave a little start. 'Goodness, I forgot to ask about Mitchell Fraser. Have you heard anything?'

'I phoned this morning. He's still giving cause for concern. There are related problems, as we know.'

Laura sighed softly. 'Let's hope he pulls through this patch.'

'And that if he does,' Antonio replied evenly, 'he'll consider the course of his life.' He paused, a slow smile tugging at his full lips. 'What time shall we expect you in the morning?'

'Seven-thirty?' she suggested with a shrug. 'Then I'll have enough time to settle Maria with your mother and be at work for eight.'

'Why not leave your car here?' he suggested casually. 'I'll drive us in and bring us home. My surgery finishes at five tomorrow. You would only have to wait a little while for me…'

Laura couldn't imagine a quicker way to set the surgery alight with gossip. Not that there was anything to gossip about but, even so, arriving and leaving with one of the doctors—no, she corrected herself mentally, with *Antonio*—could only lead to trouble. She shook her head firmly. 'Thank you, but I don't think that would be a very good idea, do you?' she said a little coolly.

Antonio's eyes flickered and a frown tugged at his forehead. 'You are worried about what people might think?'

'Aren't you?'

'No, Laura. Not especially. It's my business entirely, but I understand that from your point of view it might be…difficult.'

'I'd prefer to have my car anyway,' she replied evasively. 'Just in case.'

He nodded slowly. 'As you wish.'

She started the engine, a little unnerved at his response about not being concerned about what other people thought, or was it that somewhere deep in her unconscious there was a link to the past, to something Mark had said in the days when she'd been so madly in love that she'd gullibly swallowed everything he told her.

She'd tried so hard at first to be sensible. But Mark had been so charming, so sincere and, casting caution to the wind, she'd not really cared in the end about the other staff at school knowing she was seeing him. Maybe she had at first, when she'd tried to keep their relationship as just friendship. But then somehow it had all got out of hand and her emotions had overwhelmed common sense.

She had no one else to blame but herself, of course, not even Mark, who would have lost interest if she had maintained her refusal to have an affair. How could she have not seen the dangers or taken note of the warning signs? He'd never invited her to his home or shown her where he lived, just thought up a dozen different excuses why they should meet somewhere else or go to her flat. Even Shelley had commented on it, but still she hadn't listened. Hadn't wanted to know.

Suddenly Laura found herself stiffening and with a brief nod she turned the steering-wheel and headed the car along the drive and out of the gate. Then she felt guilty as she glanced back and saw his tall figure standing there. It wasn't fair to read anything into what Antonio had said or done. He'd only offered her a lift and probably that had been a spur-of-the-moment decision.

As she turned into the lane, she remembered the day she had given birth to Maria, recalling the fear that her baby was to be born on the roadside. And yet, amidst it all, she'd had the gut feeling she'd been in safe hands. She hadn't really registered much about Antonio then, except for his eyes, which she would have had to have been blind not to notice. Now, as she'd grown to know him a little better, had that gut feeling changed?

She simply didn't know. The last glimpse she had of him was of a tall figure, hands scrunched down in pockets, dark head tilted as he watched her car disappear.

The following day, Laura was up very early and put on her uniform so that she wouldn't have to waste time changing at work. She fed and dressed Maria and packed all her daughter's things, making notes for Signora Dallori, as she had done for Sue Kemp on that first day at the crèche.

Signora Dallori met her at the front door of Antonio's house and took her upstairs to a study that Laura could only think of as wildly Italian. There was a wonderful view over the sea and the walls were crammed with photographs. Dark-eyed, olive-skinned people, bearing a heart-thudding likeness to Antonio. Children with mops of black hair, gorgeous eyes and wide, friendly smiles.

'My family,' Signora Dallori said half-apologetically, as she followed Laura's gaze. 'Antonio is forced to add a new photograph each time I visit.' She looked back at Laura and inclined her head. 'Don't worry about Maria. Antonio has a family bedroom with bunk beds and a cot for my grandchildren's visits. If she's sleepy, she can rest there.'

'Thank you,' Laura said. 'I'm very grateful.'

'Enjoy your day.' The older woman stretched out her arms and Laura placed Maria in them. Maria blew bubbles happily. 'You see, we are friends already.'

Laura offered her thanks once more, then made her way down the pine staircase to the hall below where Antonio was waiting.

He was dressed for work in a formal white shirt and dark, elegant trousers, and her tummy tightened as she inhaled the tang of bitter-sweet lemons that she would always associate now with Canzone del Mare.

'She'll be fine,' he reassured her, laying his hand under her arm. 'I guarantee Maria will be spoiled.'

Laura lifted her shoulders on a little sigh, her skin shivering where he touched her. 'I'm sure she will.'

'Are you sure I can't drive you?' he asked as they walked outside, his expressive dark eyes, fringed by luxuriant ebony lashes, resting on her.

'No. Thank you.' She glanced up as she heard laughter drift from a window, both Antonio's mother's and Maria's.

'You see, you have no worries and neither do I,' he murmured softly.

She caught the drift of his cologne on the breeze and she made herself walk quickly to her car, her senses in uproar at the assault of so much male virility first thing in the morning.

She was thankful for the rush at work. Becky didn't have time to chat and neither did Michelle, who was on Reception duty that morning. She knew that Antonio wouldn't say anything about Maria and his mother—at least, she didn't think he'd have any reason to as he knew by now her feelings on the subject.

But at the coffee-break mid-morning, news of the rescue of Mitchell Fraser had reached everyone's ears and Becky was eager to hear the details. Laura omitted to mention that she'd helped Antonio with the CPR, just that she'd watched from Molly's café. Even some of the patients had heard about it and so the theme of the day was Mitchell Fraser.

Then, thankfully, Mrs Frost came in with yet another problem and Becky looked relieved when Laura said she'd take her. It was nothing serious, but Laura gave the woman's arthritis some consideration and, with a little of the current news to satisfy her curiosity, she was on her way again quite happily.

Laura didn't see Antonio at lunchtime, but she rang Signora Dallori from the privacy of her mobile to hear that Maria had fallen asleep in her buggy, just as she did after lunch at the crèche.

The afternoon passed so quickly, she could hardly believe it was four-thirty, and a flicker of anticipation went through her as she prepared to leave.

'I forgot to ask—how's Maria?' Becky stopped her as she gathered her bag, ready to escape. 'You had to leave early last Thursday, didn't you?'

'Oh, yes.' Laura nodded, colouring slightly. 'She's much better.'

'They get all sorts of funny things when they start crèche and school,' Becky said and proceeded to give Laura a potted history of her little boy's ills. But Laura didn't mind. She was just relieved she didn't ask any more about Maria. 'See you on Thursday, then,' Becky said eventually. 'My day off tomorrow—thank goodness. It's really hard to get back into the routine after a holiday, don't you find?'

'Mmm.' Laura nodded. 'Enjoy your day off.' Laura made a swift exit and even drove out of the car park as though she was going to the crèche and not on the outward bound road to the cliffs. Becky was a sweetie, but if she got the merest hint of what was going on, Laura would never live it down.

The pattern was set for the rest of the week. Each morning Laura took Maria to Canzone del Mare and each afternoon she collected her, remaining to stay for a cup of tea with Signora Dallori. Laura enjoyed their chats and Antonio's mother delighted in telling her what they had done that day.

By Friday, Maria's spots had vanished and her little face under her dark crop of hair was a soft shade of creamy pink. There was no doubt in Laura's mind that she would be well enough to go to the crèche the following week.

'Your son told me he is taking you to London tomorrow,' Laura said on Friday evening as she collapsed the buggy and stowed it in the boot.

Signora Dallori smiled as she held Maria in her arms, waiting for Laura to finish loading the car. 'Yes, we are going to stay with the English half of our family—my husband's brother and his wife. My niece Gabrielle has just become engaged. As they live in London, we can combine a visit to them.'

'I hope you have a lovely time.' Laura reached out and took Maria. 'Mrs Dallori, I'm so grateful for your help this week.'

'And I am grateful for yours. I shall miss Maria. She is such good company.' She paused, her dark eyes moving slowly over Laura's face. 'Would you allow me to have her for one day more, before I return to Italy?'

'Why…yes, if you'd like,' Laura said, in surprise. 'But will you have time?'

'I shall look forward to it.'

Laura was still thinking about this when, five minutes later, she realized that she was running low on petrol. In the rush this morning, she'd forgotten to stop at her local garage and so she took the road back into Charbourne town centre and pulled up in the nearest garage.

Checking her purse, she was about to climb out of the car when her hand froze on the doorhandle. A dark-coloured four-wheel-drive had paused in the road opposite, its indicator flashing as it crept slowly forward. The driver's attention was fixed on the steady flow of traffic coming from his left in the one-way system, and as a car stopped to let him through he lifted his hand in acknowledgement.

Laura licked her dry lips, her gaze fixed on the young woman who sat next to Antonio. She was dark-haired and very attractive, and Laura recognized her instantly. It was the girl she'd seen sitting in the chair by Antonio's desk on the day that she'd walked in, unintentionally disturbing them.

Something fierce and painful tugged at Laura's ribs, a sensation of impending doom, which was absolutely ridiculous, she told herself angrily. Why should she be feeling this way? What right had she to make any judgement on Antonio? But even as she thought that, she knew that every bone in her body was reacting to what she saw.

Antonio turned to his passenger and smiled, and there was something in his expression and the woman's response that made Laura take a sharp breath. In the brief moments she had to study them, Laura knew that the relationship was not as she had thought. Doctor and patient they weren't—not unless her eyes deceived her. And that, really, left little else to the imagination.

Laura sat very still, her heart thudding in her chest as she tried to ignore the strong feelings inside her. Why should she feel like this? What could possibly generate such a disturbance that her hands felt damp and a little shaky and her legs seemed to have gone to jelly?

She watched, unable to drag her eyes away as the vehicle slipped into the queue of traffic and within minutes was just a tiny speck on Laura's horizon.

Somehow she managed to fill the car with petrol and pay and drive home. Her mind felt as though it was waterlogged, unable to move left or right or up or down, and each time she tried, the vision came back of Antonio and the woman beside him.

Totally unreasonable.

Irrational.

As she took Maria into Sea Breeze and tried everything in the book to occupy her mind and regain some form of control, she knew it was useless to try to block out what had happened.

Not that she could do anything about it, she accepted later that evening as she kissed Maria goodnight. She had allowed Antonio to become important to her in a way that she would never have believed. And this, despite all she had told herself, all she had vowed not to do, she had done.

Not that it had anything to do with Antonio this week. Since their last conversation he had barely stopped to talk to her at work and she had been grateful that he hadn't. They had kept the arrangement low-key. Which was what she'd wanted—and had made it plain to him—and it had worked well.

But as she wandered along the hall and into the dining room and gazed at the table where they had sat that night, she felt a hateful pang of jealousy claw at her ribs.

She missed everything that had made up her world over the last few days—the soft sunlight and enchanting atmosphere of the house on the cliffs, the hospitality and friendliness of Signora Dallori. Most of all, she missed the warmth of Antonio's special smile—the same kind of smile that he had given the dark-haired woman—as Laura had met him each morning at Canzone del Mare.

CHAPTER SIX

OVER the next few weeks, the centre got busier with tourists and Laura was grateful for the hard and sometimes exhausting hours at work, which were at least a distraction from her personal agenda. Not that she had much of one, she sometimes thought, since the days were passing so rapidly and if she wasn't at work then she was with Maria and trying to smarten up Sea Breeze as best as she could.

At least when she was at work she was totally absorbed and as Becky was eager to return to her two days a week Laura began to shoulder a greater responsibility of patients.

Antonio seemed to pass through her life like a shadow, catching her eye briefly with a smile or flying out on his calls and raising his hand, but rarely pausing for more. Each day, Canzone del Mare seemed a million light years away. Maybe, she thought, she had blown the whole experience out of proportion. Perhaps Antonio had never intended more than just to be helpful and she'd worried unnecessarily that her space might be threatened.

As if fate was teaching her a little lesson, Antonio rarely approached her and when he did, it was always with a few words of easy, but not intimate conversation. More often than not, they were shared with the other staff and even Becky stopped teasing her.

April turned into an unusually warm May and Laura found herself settling into a comfortable routine. Maria loved the crèche and the last few stubborn spots had disappeared from her feet.

It was at the end of one overcast Wednesday morning, when Laura was helping Mo Fielding with her antenatal clinic, that Antonio appeared, casting his eyes around the treatment room as he walked in.

'Hi, there,' he called, slanting her a grin that sent her heart into a series of uncontrollable skitters. 'Busy still or are you finished?'

Laura managed a smile. 'I'm finished till two-fifteen. Mo's just gone for lunch. Did you want her?'

'No, but I…er…do need a favour.' He frowned, coming in and closing the door behind him. He dominated the room, his height and presence making her feel vulnerable to his masculinity.

'What is it?' she asked as her hand went up to sweep her golden brown hair from her face and tuck the wing behind her ear. Her lashes fluttered down as her green eyes tried not to lock with his, because once she looked into them, she knew her response would be humiliatingly apparent.

'I have a patient with me…' He lifted his shoulders, which were hidden under a gorgeous pale blue silk shirt, and sighed deeply. 'A teenager, fifteen, taking her GCSEs—and she's pregnant.'

Suddenly Laura looked up. 'Fifteen?'

'Not sixteen until summer. And she won't say who the father is. All she'll say is that they took precautions, but there was a mishap with the condom. She's terrified of her parents finding out.' He lowered one muscular thigh to the desk and perched there, folding his arms across his chest.

'Because they'd want to know who he is,' Laura guessed.

'And Bethany is aware of the implications of underage sex.'

'What does she want to do?'

'Well, in her words…her parents will go bananas if she tells them. So, please, can I do something to stop it? I tried talking to her about her choices, that she should understand what a termination means and also what a pregnancy involves.' He crooked an eyebrow. 'She's already in the second trimester, just over sixteen weeks.'

'She's certain of her dates?'

'She seems so, yes.'

'And she didn't consider the morning-after pill?'

'I think she took a chance that it would be OK.'

'Poor love,' Laura sighed. 'When did she realize she was pregnant?'

'Her menstruation cycle is a bit dippy, but then last week she couldn't ignore it any longer and told a friend who advised her to take an over-the-counter test.' He rubbed his hand slowly over his chin and made a little click with his tongue. 'The thing is, she's so scared she hasn't thought about the baby—or a termination—in real values. All she's focusing on is her parents and what they'll say or do. She's the only daughter and clearly they have expectations of her doing well in her exams.'

Laura nodded slowly. 'How can I help?'

'I explained we were running an antenatal clinic this afternoon so I asked her if she'd like to talk to our nurse. I think she'd welcome some female input about her pregnancy. She certainly didn't object to the suggestion.'

Laura lifted her shoulders on a sigh. 'I'll speak to her, of course, but I'm not certain that I can do very much.'

'Thanks, Laura.' He smiled and his eyes creased deliciously, and all the conflicting sensations rushed back as Laura gazed unguardedly into the dark, fluidly sensual eyes. A tremor ran right through her and she fought for composure as her roller-coaster pulse went out of control.

'What's the girl's full name?' she asked, trying to put aside her feelings as he told her it was Bethany Graham and that he'd taken her along to the little rest room at the end of the hall where there was a comfortable easy chair and magazines.

A few moments later Laura found herself making a cup of tea in the office, sliding a biscuit onto the saucer and taking it along. Bethany looked unbelievably young in her uniform, curled in the easy chair, her head hanging and her long brown hair falling over her face.

Laura put the cup of tea on the coffee-table and sat beside her. 'Hi, Bethany, I'm Laura, the practice nurse.' She smiled, not wanting to crowd the girl or make her feel she had to talk, but Bethany gave an imperceptible nod, tears springing to her eyes, and suddenly she was in floods, as though the sight of an impartial face had released all her emotions.

Laura reached under the table and drew out a packet of tissues, tearing several away and tucking them gently into Bethany's hand.

Laura waited as the sobs subsided and as Bethany gave a shaky sigh, blowing her nose and pushing the tissues into her cuff, Laura handed her the cup of tea. 'Have a sip, Bethany. Tea always helps. My little girl loves it. It's the first thing we do when I go home. I make tea and we sit and drink it in the garden. Of course, she has her beaker to drink from. She's a little dangerous with a cup yet— most of it goes over the grass. Which is why we take it into the garden!'

Bethany shook back her hair and took the cup of tea. Under the long strands of heavy brown hair, Bethany was a pretty girl, with wide, intelligent, bright blue eyes, though they were red-rimmed now and very frightened. She had a full, sweet mouth and Laura's heart clenched. Just a child yet.

'Do you live on your own with your daughter?' Bethany asked, and Laura nodded.

'Yes, I'm a single parent.'

Bethany sat up a little, a frown creasing her forehead. 'Don't you have any parents?'

'No, they died, I'm afraid, when I was young, and my aunt brought me up.'

'That must have been awful,' Bethany croaked.

'Well, it would have been if it hadn't been for my aunt, who was absolutely brilliant.'

'But she's not alive either,' Bethany guessed. 'Not if you live on your own.'

'No, she isn't. And I do miss her.'

Bethany was silent for a while, then sipped her tea. 'How old is your baby?'

'Nearly eight months now.'

Bethany nodded thoughtfully. 'What happens to her whilst you're at work?'

'She's cared for at the college crèche. I was worried at first that she might not like it but, in fact, she loves being with other children. Still, I can't wait to see her when I finish work. And I'm really looking forward to doing things with her in the summer. There's a playground on the beach close to where we live. It's not open yet, but as soon as it is, we're going there.'

Bethany was silent for a long while until finally she finished her tea and blew her nose again. 'What's the best thing about having a baby?' she asked, and Laura told her how Maria had become the focus of her life and how it had helped her to mature in ways she'd thought never existed.

Bethany uncurled her legs and sighed. 'At least you have a job and stuff. I shan't be able to finish my exams, not if I have the baby.'

'Maybe not right now,' Laura said, 'but at a later date you could take them. There are all sorts of schemes to help people with further education. The Family Planning Association are very helpful and other societies and groups have been set up especially to help with parental concerns.'

'But my dad will kill me if he finds out,' Bethany protested, as she looked tearful again.

'Do you get on well?' Laura asked, and the young girl nodded.

'Normally, yes. Although they're very strict about boy-friends. They don't know I've been seeing…' She stopped, flushing. 'It's just that I don't want to disappoint them.'

'They'll probably go through a mixture of emotions, as you have,' Laura agreed. 'But only because they're protective of you and because it'll be a shock at first. But then they'll want to help and support you and, together with other people who'll be able to advise you, you'll be able to come to a decision.'

'So you really think they'll understand?'

'Yes, I do,' Laura said gently. 'I wish I'd had my aunt to talk to when I became pregnant. I felt very alone and I think I'd have understood that her reaction—however upsetting it was at first—was because she cared for me.'

Twenty minutes later, Laura and Bethany walked together along the hall and Laura felt a ripple of uncertainty as Bethany paused outside Antonio's slightly open door.

'Do you work here all the time?' Bethany asked.

'Yes, except for Saturday.'

'I might see you again, then.'

'I'd like that.' Laura smiled, her eyes meeting Bethany's, and she watched the girl turn and walk into Antonio's room.

Laura walked slowly back along the corridor, her heart going out to Bethany and to all young women who found themselves in such a dilemma. She'd been there herself and, though she'd never really considered a termination, at times she had wondered if she could cope with the life-changing decision she had finally made.

It had all been worth it in the end—even the despair of her relationship with Mark had taken second place to the wonder and joy of Maria's birth. But at least she had been old enough to have some experience of life. At fifteen, what chance had Bethany ever had to prepare for this?

Laura walked back to her treatment room, her appetite for her lunch having disappeared. It was nearly two anyway and her list began at two-fifteen. So she tidied her room, hoping with all her heart that Bethany would find the courage to share her predicament with her parents and that they, in turn, would set aside their fear and anger for compassion.

Later that afternoon, after the clinic, Laura was checking that her list for the next day was complete when Antonio knocked on her door. She'd had no chance to think about

Bethany, not with the antenatals in progress, but as she saw him enter, her thoughts flew back to the young girl.

'I don't know what you said but, whatever it was, it went home,' Antonio told her as he entered.

'You mean Bethany? In what way?' Her skin flushed as she breathed in the trickle of scent that filled the room.

'She said she realized there was more to—her words—"babies and stuff" and that she thought her mother might be less angry than her father and she might tell her tonight.'

'Do we know the parents at all?' Laura asked.

'I checked that out while Bethany was with you. Mrs Graham is on Ravi Chandra's list. Which is why, I suppose, Bethany came to me and not Ravi.'

'That makes sense,' Laura said. 'So what happens now?'

'After she's broken the news to her mum—*hopefully*—then we can set up a few meetings—counsellors, social workers and, of course, an obstetrician if she's keeping the child. If not, then...' he shook his head slowly '...we'll go along different lines.'

'Fifteen,' Laura sighed. 'And in the middle of her exams.'

'Plus the problem of the boyfriend.'

Laura frowned. 'She must think a lot of him to want to shield him.'

Antonio nodded, then slid her a slow, intimate smile. 'Love conquers all, so they say, and maybe she's underestimating him. Maybe he'll turn up and help her to shoulder the responsibility.' His smile had her weakening at the knees and she tried not to read anything into it. Most women would have done anything for that smile, she thought as a vision of the woman with dark hair appeared in her mind.

'There is one more piece of news,' he murmured as she lifted her shoulder-bag and slid it over her arm. 'If you're leaving, I'll tell you on our way out.'

Laura realized she had no reason not to accompany him, but as they walked into Reception Michelle looked across at them curiously. 'Goodnight, Dr Dallori, bye, Laura,' she called, and Laura waved casually, leaving Antonio to say a more leisurely goodnight.

Laura felt the soft air on her face, cooling the flush that had covered her skin as she'd tried to escape. Her car was parked next to his and she waited for him to catch up, his dark eyes claiming hers as he arrived beside her and leaned against her car.

'I forgot,' he said teasingly, 'that we shouldn't be seen together.'

'It's not that at all,' she flustered. 'I just don't want to be late for Maria.'

'I'm sorry, I didn't realize I was delaying you.' He shrugged but he seemed in no hurry to let her go.

'What were you going to tell me?' she prompted, and he gave another little grin.

'I thought you'd be interested to know that Mitchell Fraser was discharged a week ago. The hospital tried to make him a follow-up appointment at Outpatients. However, he refused, saying he'd visit his GP.'

'But he hasn't seen you?' Laura guessed.

'Oh, yes, he came in earlier and thanked us for what we did. He said he'd merely missed his footing and cracked his head before falling into the water. I knew differently, of course. The hospital had sent me his results. No evidence of trauma to the skull, but his blood results are a nightmare. His alcohol level was sky high on the day. Later results showed raised cholesterol and blood sugar, and further tests are needed on an ECG result.'

'Will he take up the appointment now?'

'Lord only knows. I would have thought the drowning episode would have scared him. But he took it so lightly— despite my ramming it down his throat that he's got to make changes in his life.'

'He's in denial of his condition,' Laura said slowly, then, remembering Maria, she glanced at her watch. 'Is it really that time? I must fly.' She hurriedly slid her key into the lock.

'You won't be doing much flying in this,' he said with a smile, crooking an eyebrow at her car.

'It's roadworthy.' She smiled sweetly. 'Not quite in Mitchell Fraser's league, but at least I'm safe.' He nodded absently as she climbed in and shut the door, winding down her window with a creak.

'That's the big worry,' he muttered grimly. 'He fell off a boat last time, but what if he drinks and drives and wraps his car around a tree?'

'You can't run his life for him,' she said as she started her car. 'You've warned him, and if he's got any sense, he'll listen to you.' Her foot hovered on the accelerator as she raised her eyes to his until finally he straightened and stepped back.

'Say hello to Maria from me,' he murmured, and she looked up into the concerned, sun-bronzed features that made her heart tumble and twist until she dragged her eyes back to the road and what she should be doing.

Still, she didn't remember much of the drive to the crèche. Only that somehow she must have got there on autopilot.

Antonio was genuinely worried about Mitchell Fraser. As he was for all his patients, which was, she thought on a decidedly shuddery inner sigh, all part of his attraction. He even remembered to ask about Maria, and it touched her. But if she tried to read meaning into his every word, she was crazy.

But, then, maybe she had been a little crazy since the first day she had met him eight months ago. And somehow she'd got addicted to the feeling of craziness.

That weekend Laura rang the estate agents and told them she was willing to reconsider the selling price of Sea Breeze. That, she hoped, plus the small changes she was making, would encourage interest. The agents told her, fine, they'd offer the new details to interested parties.

So she replaced the carpet in the first-floor room, managing to fit it herself because it was light and cheap, but it did look good when she'd finished. She had a little time to herself because Mrs Kent had her granddaughter to stay and had said she was going to take her along the promenade and had wondered if Laura would let her take Maria in the buggy.

Mrs Kent's granddaughter was sixteen and wanted to be a nanny. She loved babies and so on the Saturday afternoon Laura had waved Maria goodbye under her little sun canopy and Mrs Kent and Rachel had sauntered off to the beach. It was an overcast day, with a soft, cool breeze, so, having taken up the old carpet and laying the new, Laura sat in the garden and wondered if she dared start decorating.

She was halfway through the first wall when the phone rang. Scraping her hands down the sides of her jeans, she picked up the phone in the hall.

'Laura? This is Elena Dallori.'

Laura clutched the telephone. 'How are you, Mrs Dallori?'

'I'm fine, thank you, Laura. And Maria?'

'She's very well. All her spots have gone. Did you have a good time in London?'

'Yes, but I was pleased to come back to Canzone. I miss the sea, you know. Laura, it would be so nice to see Maria again before I go home. And, of course, you. I would suggest tomorrow, but perhaps I have left it too late and you are busy.'

Laura thought rapidly. Did she really want to expose herself to such sweet torture again? Canzone del Mare had begun to fade in her mind, just a little, although hearing Elena Dallori's warm voice brought back so much. If she visited again, it would take days to get over, and the more pleasant the experience, the worse it would be.

'You are busy, of course,' Elena said as Laura's silence

lengthened. 'I am sure you have far better things to do than visit an old lady.'

'No, not at all,' Laura answered, hating herself for being so weak. 'I'm only decorating.'

'Decorating? In that case, I can be of use. Perhaps Maria would like to spend the day with me whilst you continue?'

Laura chewed fiercely on her lip. If only she could say no, politely but firmly...something, apparently, she simply couldn't get her head around doing when it came to Elena Dallori.

'If you're sure,' she heard herself accepting. Oh, what a failure she was! Laura rang off and leaned against the wall. What had she done? Why had she done it? But it was too late now. She had made the arrangement and she'd have to stick to it.

Just about every negative thought that could enter Laura's mind did. She painted furiously in an effort not to give space to the endless possibilities, and when Mrs Kent returned with Maria, she offered her neighbour and Rachel a cup of tea and sat in the garden with them, talking at length, so that she wouldn't have to fall back on her endless doubts.

But, of course, she did eventually. And after Maria was asleep, she prowled restlessly around the place, picking up her paint brush and adding touches here and there. But eventually she decided it was more exhausting to stop her thoughts than give them freedom.

So she sat at the table in the dining room and gazed out across the bay, absorbing the tranquillity. There must be hundreds of good, solid excuses that weren't excuses but were quite legitimate...if only she could think of them!

She thought until her head ached and she had to massage her temples to ease the pain, scolding herself for being a fool. But even now her traitorous mind clawed back memories of Antonio sitting here, his eyes glimmering like deep, dark pools, his smile sending a pang of yearning ripping through her. Every cell in her body weakened, grasping hungrily at the memory until she stood up, banking it down fiercely as she marched up the stairs into decorating oblivion.

Sunday dawned warm and bright and Laura opted for shorts and T-shirts for both her and Maria. Her thoughts tumbled erratically as she hurriedly scrunched her long hair up into a cap, its peak gently softening the sunlight on her face.

The shorts were easy-on-the-eye denim and fitted her narrow hips perfectly, her long, softly tanned legs looking their best in casual gear. In London she'd had one major shopping spree before Maria had been born and had managed to mix and match some of her T-shirts with Maria's. The cool lime greens and lilacs were dotted with little bears and honeypots and they'd been a ghastly expense, but she'd loved them.

'How do we look, sweetie?' Laura asked Maria before they set off, and Maria stabbed her thumb appreciatively on the biggest honeypot on her chest and gurgled, crinkling her nose.

Laura chuckled, forgetting for a moment her unease. It was a lovely day and too good to worry about something she couldn't alter. So she bundled her things into the car, pressed Maria's little sunhat on her head and set off for Canzone.

By the time she drove in through the gate and parked, she had decided that perhaps Antonio might not even be at home. The four-wheel-drive wasn't there. And Elena Dallori hadn't mentioned her son...

Laura paused, looking up at the flawless blue sky and a sun that was just breaking through the haze. She had almost convinced herself Antonio was absent when the impressive front oak door opened and he stepped out.

Her heart beat wildly as he walked towards them. His long, muscular legs emerged from baggy blue shorts as he ambled casually over the sand-coloured pebbles, his arms swinging by his sides. His head was slightly tilted, the sleek, thick curve of black hair catching the sunlight and remaining unadulterated ebony.

A thousand confused messages flew back to her brain as the tall, unbelievably sexy figure in a white T-shirt came slowly towards her, a welcoming smile on his face.

Maria squealed when she saw him and his smile turned into soft laughter. 'Hi, little one! You recognized me!' he called, and stretched out his arms, their smooth muscles showered in silky jet black spirals of hair.

Laura swallowed. 'I wasn't certain if you'd be here.' She hesitated. 'Or even if your mother mentioned I was coming. And when I didn't see your car...'

'It's in the garage,' he said with a throaty chuckle as he opened her door and waited for her to climb out. 'What, no decorating overalls?' He arched an eyebrow as his eyes went slowly over her T-shirt and shorts, taking an eternity to settle on her face. Laura felt goose-bumps flow over her as he added playfully, 'So you've time for a coffee and a few words with *Mamma*—and *then* we can go.'

'We?' she repeated, her green-gold eyes widening.

Antonio gave a little nod, disappearing into the car and releasing Maria from her seat. 'Today, *bambina*,' he said with a chuckle as he hugged her to his chest, then lifted her above his head in his strong arms, 'I'm going to help your mummy while you are in the safest of hands.'

'Help *me*?' Laura said in astonishment.

As Maria's laughter filled the morning air, he nodded.

'But...but I can't possibly—' she began, but her protest was lost as he curled Maria into the crook of his arm, slid a hand under her elbow and propelled her towards the house.

Ten minutes later she was sitting on the terrace, watching Elena pour the most delicious filter coffee into her cup. And half an hour later, with Maria comfortably settled at Canzone del Mare, she was sitting beside Antonio in the front seat of his four-wheel-drive as they flew down the hill to Sea Breeze.

CHAPTER SEVEN

'I'VE not had a guided tour,' Antonio said with a grin that made Laura feel about sixteen. 'Does voluntary labour qualify for one?'

They were standing in the hall and looking up the stairs, and Laura was wondering if she had flipped. Fancy agreeing to let him come and help her! She must be mad, or something else—maybe hypnotized! Not only had she given in to Signora Dallori yesterday, but now she had to contend with the fact that Antonio would be here all day, working alongside her.

Idiot that she was, she'd made some feeble protest, then fallen like a pack of cards into letting him come. And what's more, using his car! So she was stuck, having to rely on him for transport for the day.

Not that it was the end of the world, not having her car. It just felt odd to be reliant again. In a vague way, her car was her symbol of independence and he'd tried once before to persuade her to leave it behind.

Now she had—and she felt weird. He was here, in Sea Breeze, changed from those mind-boggling shorts into close-fitting jeans and a casual shirt, ready for work.

So he said.

But how was she going to get any work done? Male distraction wasn't quite what she needed at the moment— not if she wanted to finish the first floor in time for the hordes of interested buyers she hoped would soon be flooding through the front door.

And he wasn't just an ordinary male. On a scale of one to ten, she thought as she inhaled those fateful lemons, he'd probably be—

'Laura?'

'Oh, sorry. Um…yes, of course I'll show you around. Not that's there's a lot to see. And I've only half finished the first floor.' She led the way upstairs.

'Half finished is pretty good going,' he said as they peered into the room that she'd just finished. The cheap dark blue carpet looked pretty good, she thought in relief. She'd washed the curtains and the blinds and had polished the furniture and changed the lampshades. 'Great.' He nodded. 'How long did this take you?'

'Since before Easter really,' she had to admit.

'One down and how many to go?' He frowned.

'There's four on this floor, plus loos and bathrooms. Two won't need painting, but they'll have to be freshened up. I'm working on a budget.'

'So where do you want me to start?'

She laughed, her eyes twinkling. 'Take your pick.'

'Where will you be?'

'Next room along.'

'Will it fit two of us, or will I get under your feet?'

'Not if you're doing the walls. There's a cupboard in the corner I need to strip. Aunt M. must have papered over it in a moment of desperation. The wood's good underneath. Anyway, help yourself to paint. I'll just change.'

She flew down the stairs and tugged on her paint-splattered jeans and T-shirt, then hurried back up again. Her cheeks were flushed and her pulse was racing as she entered the room breathlessly. But he just slid her a smile, which did nothing at all to slow her pulse, and continued to work easily on the walls, his shoulders looking ridiculously broad and capable under his loose shirt.

Laura forced her attention on the cupboard and it worked for the first half-hour, providing she didn't look over her shoulder. Antonio covered an area in minutes which it would have taken her hours to do, and every so often she gave in to temptation and looked round.

She could hardly believe he was here!

It all felt dreamlike.

Well, she had better pinch herself, if that was the case, and wake up. Or she'd never get any work done. When she'd soaked off all the wallpaper and scraped down to bare wood, she took the rubbish down to the bin in the kitchen and made a drink. She brought the cold orange squash up in long glasses. He drank it greedily as they sat on the bare boards of the floor, talking for a while.

'What have you done with the furniture?' he asked curiously.

'I gave the bed to Mrs Kent.' Laura sighed, even now wishing she'd kept it because of her finances. 'It felt uncomfortable and saggy. And she needed one quickly for a guest. Mr Kent came with their son and carried it back, and that's why I decided to do this room next.'

'Eight rooms are a big undertaking for one person.' He frowned. 'Couldn't you get someone in to help?'

'As I've said, I'm on a budget. And I've already brought the price down.'

'It should fetch it,' he agreed when she'd told him her asking price.

'City prices are horrendous,' she sighed, thinking of the dingy little flats she really didn't want to spend the rest of her life in. 'That's why I have the budget. So that I can put every bean into something decent.'

'Do you really want to go back to the City?' he murmured, and a little lump grew in her throat as she thought of leaving Sea Breeze. Not just leaving the guest-house really, but the sea and the sand and the air and the crèche and the medical centre. In such a short time it all had become the focus of her life.

'No and yes.' She hesitated, trying to avoid his stare. 'Aunt M. used to say that needs must. So I haven't let myself think about having what isn't practical.'

A shiver ran up her spine as his arm brushed hers. The window above them was open and the breeze stirred scents of lemon and sea and paint and she felt her tummy revolve.

He didn't take his arm away, just left it there, and she wondered how long she could stay sitting closely beside him without groaning. Or screaming. Or collapsing.

'Practical's fine.' He shrugged. 'But what about your dreams, Laura? You must have some.'

She felt the little lump in her throat swell. 'Dreams,' she whispered, 'are expensive.'

The pause was long and strained before he answered with a question. 'He hurt you, didn't he—Maria's father?'

She trapped her lip with her teeth so that she'd hang onto her control. 'He hurt Maria more. And for that I can't forgive him.'

He was silent again until he reached out and took her tightly clenched hand from her knees. He held it gently on his thigh and her mind felt as though it were in orbit, her body hanging in by a thread. Her emotions were in uproar as the soft cloth of his shirt trickled against her skin and the warm strength of his fingers enclosed her hand. 'Talk to me, Laura. Open up. Just a little bit.'

She shook her head slowly and felt the tears prick. 'It's no use,' she murmured, swallowing hard. 'I'll only make a fool of myself.' She stared at her painty jeans, terrified to look into his eyes, but his hand came across, clasped her chin and turned her head towards him.

'Look at me, Laura.'

She lifted her eyes slowly, blinking.

'I won't hurt you, I promise. I want us to be friends. And friends listen as much as they talk. Tell me about him.'

She couldn't even raise a whisper. Her heart was doing something horrendous inside her chest and her breath seemed lodged in her throat, halfway between a sob and a sigh.

Antonio squeezed her hand and nodded. 'You can do it.'

She gave a regretful smile. 'I'd rather not.'

'You never talk to *anyone*?'

She shook her head as his eyes refused to let her gaze go.

'Not even to your friend…Shelley?'

Laura swallowed. 'She…she warned me in the first place. About Mark. When I…when I got pregnant and he left, she didn't exactly say, "I told you so." But she had every right to. So I…I—'

'Put on a brave face?'

'I had to. If I wanted to keep Maria. I knew she thought it would be best…if, well, if I considered other things.' She made herself swallow. 'A termination, for instance.'

'And you didn't want that?'

'No.'

'And you didn't have any support from him?'

'He couldn't. He has a family, another life,' she murmured, a tear escaping down her cheek. She scrubbed it fiercely away with a painty cuff but he captured her hand and drew it down to his thigh, carefully wrapping both her fists into his palms.

She looked into the soft, ebony eyes that were staring into hers and suddenly she found herself telling him about Mark. The words tumbled out in disorder, a year of her life that seemed amazingly distant now. A life-changing year that had brought her to this moment in time.

Mark had been her first real relationship, a romance that had changed to certain knowledge he had been Mr Right. A young supply teacher to the school she worked at, who had persuaded her into believing he was free to love. A man who, unbeknownst to Laura, had been living a double life—a *happy* double life—with his wife and child, and from his own boredom and vanity had accepted her love and respect.

And when it had come to the choice of her pregnancy and his family, there had been no choice. He'd even questioned whether their baby was his. That was what hurt most. And that was the moment when she'd known it was over.

'You could have proved it,' Antonio said gently. 'And made him take responsibility.'

She nodded through the hot, hurtful tears. '*Made* him, yes.'

'Another road,' he guessed, 'that you didn't want to go down.'

'What was the point? He didn't love me. I had no desire to hurt his wife or son. The little boy was only five. I could have only brought further unhappiness by making them aware of what Mark had done. And to have that on my conscience would be unbearable.'

'Oh, Laura,' he sighed, and digging into his jeans he pulled out a handkerchief and dabbed her cheeks. The cloth smelt of lemons and she shivered. She gave a wobbly smile and took it and made swift repairs. Then she sniffed and a little shudder went through her.

'Here, let me look at you.' This time he turned her by the shoulders and looked into her eyes. She felt his warm palms cup them and found her knees tangling with his thighs as she tried not to think about looking a wreck. 'Thank you,' he whispered huskily, and she frowned.

'What for?'

'For talking to me.'

She smiled shakily. 'It feels odd—talking like this. I hope I don't regret it tomorrow.' Then she gave a little start. 'Or you.'

'Why should I regret it?'

'Because the conversation's been a little one-sided.' She smiled and then laughed softly. 'Unless, of course, now you'd like to put that right?'

'In which case, we won't get much work done.'

A little frown pleated her forehead. 'That hardly seems to matter.'

'What if we finish the walls and the cupboard and then talk?'

She laughed softly, her green eyes shining. 'Very clever. There won't be time. And you'll get off scot-free.'

He was laughing, too, his mouth turning up at the corners

so sexily she felt breathless again. 'Not really. I can just use it as an excuse to see you again.'

Her heart nearly burrowed out of her chest. He wanted to see her again. And, oh, lord, she wanted to see him too. Desperately, hopelessly, mindlessly, she wanted to…

But how could she have let this happen? How could she go back on her promise to herself that she wouldn't let their relationship develop? Friends, he'd said, but how dishonest of her to agree to be friends when she was aching for him like this?

Aching for his hands to slip down her arms and bring her towards him with all the strength and power that she knew was in them. To let him hold her against his chest and bring his mouth down and cover hers with those wonderful lips that were only offering friendship. How could she be so unfair, so devious, wanting one thing and accepting another?

Laura shivered under his touch. His eyes reflected her face. She looked into the reflection and saw someone else there. Someone thinking one thing and about to say another. Could she ever blame Mark again for his deception? When she was now doing the same?

'Antonio,' she faltered, 'I can't do this. I'm sorry. I've let you come here and I shouldn't have. It's my fault. This…this *friendship* you talk about—it won't work.'

'How do you know it won't?' His hands dropped slowly from her shoulders and she wriggled her hands around her knees again, distancing herself.

'Because I do.'

'Laura, you can't predict the future.'

She turned then, her eyes narrowing. 'I have to try. I have a baby—a child—a dependant. I can't let her look forward to things that won't remain a constant in her life. She's lost too much already.'

'I have no intention of taking anything from her,' he protested gently. 'She is very special to me.'

'I know. And that shouldn't be happening.' Laura scrambled to her feet. 'Antonio, it's late. We ought to go.'

He stood up, towering over her. 'Laura, you can't become a hermit. You are a modern woman living in modern times. And Maria will always have you as her constant. Her foundation. But she must have other people, too. From a child she must learn about life, providing she is allowed to do so.'

'I know that,' she began, stopping, trying to say what she really meant and yet unable to. 'Antonio, please, take me back to Canzone.'

He waited, his eyes flowing over her slowly, her skin flushing under his stare and her gaze unsteadily meeting his. She felt as though the world were shaking under her feet and she wanted it to be steady again. She wanted to retreat to that safe place she'd been in before she'd met him. Needed to be sure that she would never be out of control again, or allow her life or Maria's to be threatened.

'I'll take you,' he said at last. She fled from the room to change her clothes, telling herself it was far better this way. Far, far better now than later, when she would have compromised Maria's security and her own for a few months of something he called friendship but which would, for her, have come to mean much more.

Elena and Maria were in the little study when they arrived. They'd been for a walk with the buggy along the lane and across the cliff and Maria had pretty pink cheeks from all the fresh air.

'You'll stay to eat with us,' Elena said as she handed Maria to Laura. 'We'll sit on the terrace again.'

'I'd like to but…' Laura hesitated, aware that Antonio was beside her, looping a finger through Maria's palm. 'I still have so much to do.'

'I understand.' Elena nodded.

She could see that the older woman was disappointed and it touched her. But when she looked into Antonio's eyes, she knew she had done the right thing. She had to make a stand somewhere. She had to protect herself and Maria and she had to be fair to him.

Friendship, he had said. But the minute he'd said it, she'd known it could never be. There were too many emotions whipped up inside her. Too many feelings that she was trying to hide. Feelings that frightened her and threatened her. And even if it was only friendship for him, she could never claim that certainty.

'I am leaving for Italy next week,' Antonio's mother said regretfully. 'I must say goodbye.' She leaned forward and kissed Maria on both cheeks. Laura repeated again her thanks and wished Elena a safe journey back to Italy. Then, with a final embrace, Laura left the little study.

Antonio folded the buggy into the boot of the car and lifted Maria into her seat, chuckling softly as Maria grasped his hair.

Laura watched, her heart quickening as he gently disentangled himself.

'I don't want your mother to think me ungrateful,' Laura said as he closed the car door and turned to her. 'She's been so sweet to us.'

'She doesn't think that way,' he told her, and smiled. 'Hospitality is a way of life in Italy.'

Laura looked up, knowing she could so easily give in. 'Thank you for your help.'

'I did very little.'

'You very nearly finished the room. You probably would have if I hadn't wasted time.'

'I would like to waste more time,' he told her with a smile that started all the wrong things moving inside her. 'May I, one day?'

'Antonio—' she began, but he reached up and pressed a finger on her lips.

'Don't answer, just let's…wait and see.' He bent slowly and, drawing her against him, kissed her, his lips moving experimentally over hers and then lifting an inch as his eyes claimed her shocked ones with an expression that made her knees buckle.

For a moment she felt the raw, physical impact of the kiss, even though it had been brief. More, it was his eyes, the way they seemed to suck her down into their depths, and that terrified her.

She felt so weak, so vulnerable—and so attracted.

'Drive home safely,' he whispered huskily, releasing her, and she grasped blindly for the door and opened it. This time she didn't look in her mirror toward the setting sun dipping behind the rosy tiled roof of Canzone. She wasn't brave enough. She just drove on, aware of Maria's contented murmurings and the crazy hammering of her heart.

During a coffee-break on Monday, Ravi Chandra came into Laura's room.

'It's Louise Graham,' Ravi told her. 'If you're free, she would like to speak about Bethany.'

'Is Bethany here, too?' Laura asked, but Ravi shook her head. Her long, shining black hair was tied back at the nape of her neck, two dark wings falling softly against her dusky skin.

'She's at school,' she explained as they walked along the hall.

'How did Mrs Graham take the news?' Laura asked.

'She wants to know who the father is,' Ravi said. 'Which is only to be expected.'

'Have you spoken to Dr Dallori?'

'He's on call, unfortunately.' Ravi shrugged under her smooth red silk blouse.

They walked into the room and Mrs Graham looked up. It was clear she was very angry, her pale face strained as she sat stiffly on her chair. 'I demand to know everything my daughter told you,' she said immediately, looking at Laura with accusing eyes. 'Especially the name of the person responsible.'

'I can't help you,' Laura said as she took a chair. 'Bethany just explained she was worried about her exams.'

'So she should be,' Louise Graham retorted. 'Don't you realize she's not sixteen yet? She can't have a baby! It's just not right for a fifteen-year-old. She's a baby herself. And, besides, what will her father say? You had no right to fill her head with fantasies about babies.'

Just then a tap came on the door and it opened. Antonio entered, his dark eyes going to Laura and then to the other women. 'Sorry I wasn't here, Mrs Graham—'

'You had no right to influence my daughter!' she broke in fiercely. 'Bethany should have come to us, not to a complete stranger.'

Antonio closed the door, scooping a chair from the corner of the room to place it beside Louise. He crossed one leg over another and said quietly, 'It was through Nurse Bright that your daughter did confide in you.'

'What do you mean?' The woman's suspicious eyes went back to Laura.

'Bethany was afraid about what her father would say. Nurse Bright did nothing more than spend a few moments chatting with your daughter in order to reassure her.'

'So that's what you call it,' the woman replied aggressively. 'I call it interfering. You have no idea how much we've sacrificed for Bethany. She's studied hard for her exams and then she lets some…some *stranger* do this to her, and her life is ruined.' Pulling a tissue from her bag, she dabbed her eyes with shaking hands. 'He should be made to pay for what he's done.'

'Which is probably why Bethany is shielding him,' Antonio said uncompromisingly.

'So you know who it is?' Mrs Graham demanded angrily.

'We have no idea,' Antonio assured her. 'At the moment your daughter needs support and understanding, and I explained that there are people who can help and advise her.

She needs to know all the facts before she comes to a decision.'

'*What* decision?' Louise exclaimed, her face horrified. 'She can't have a baby and that's the end of it! It's just not possible. Where would she go? We haven't got room. Her brother's only eight—there's just no way we could have a baby in the house. And I'm working full time. I mean, it's just ridiculous.'

'I'd like you to speak to the social worker,' Antonio said, and crooked an eyebrow.

'Why? There's no point. I know what we have to do.'

'Have you considered the effects of a termination? It will, after all, be your daughter, not you, who undergoes the procedure and its long-term effects.'

At this, Louise shuddered, collapsing in the chair. She lowered her head in her hands and was silent. Ravi Chandra stood up and walked to the basin in the corner of the room. She poured a glass of water and brought it over and Louise drank a few sips.

Antonio stood up. 'We'll talk again, Mrs Graham,' he said, and glanced at Laura. She stood up, too, and said goodbye, but Bethany's mother ignored her.

Antonio joined Laura in the hall. 'Don't take what she said to heart,' he said gently as they walked back to her room. 'She's finding it hard to accept what's happened.'

'I don't seem to have helped Bethany at all,' Laura said doubtfully. 'In fact, I may have made things worse.'

'Why do you say that?'

'Perhaps I shouldn't have spoken so freely about Maria.'

He shrugged dismissively. 'You started Bethany thinking. And that can only be a good thing. It's important she makes a decision she's comfortable with.'

Laura sighed softly. 'And there's Mr Graham to tell yet. Poor Bethany.'

'Indeed.' He touched her lightly on her shoulder. 'Is Becky in today?'

'No, she's off sick.'

'So you've a busy day ahead,' he said, his dark eyes reassuring as he smiled. 'Don't worry about the Grahams. They'll be OK.'

Laura tried a little smile and wished she felt as confident, then she heard steps coming along the corridor. Antonio's hand was still on her shoulder and some involuntary action made her step quickly away.

Michelle and Mrs Frost approached and Michelle raised her eyes as they came towards her. 'Laura, Mrs Frost isn't booked in, but you have a few minutes before your next patient. Could you see her?'

Laura smiled. 'Hello, Mrs Frost.'

'My dear, I don't know where I am. I'm all at twos and threes, and look at these.' She held out her shaky hands. 'I simply can't stop them.'

'Go along in, we'll see what we can do,' Laura said, and Michelle beamed her a smile as she ushered the elderly lady into the room.

'Thank you,' she mouthed, before glancing at Antonio and turning back along the corridor.

'I'll see you later,' Antonio said, his smile making Laura feel as though she was suddenly able to contend with a dozen Mrs Frosts and, indeed, any other eventualities that lurked ominously in the waiting room.

She nodded, meeting his eyes, recalling the way his lips had covered hers as he'd held her yesterday outside Canzone. She had spent the whole evening thinking about that moment and the words he'd whispered. *Don't answer yet. Let's wait and see.* Mere inches had separated them but a whole raft of doubts had been swept away as she'd looked into his eyes and the doubts had been replaced with desire.

Desire so strong she would have melted against him there and then if hadn't been for Maria. And what a fool he would have thought her if she had. For all her protests and her refusal to become involved, her body had been saying quite the opposite. What confused messages had she been sending Antonio?

If she'd given in to that kiss, what would have happened?

You might have got to know him better, a voice inside her head replied. What would be wrong in that? He might not be like Mark. You're judging before you know...

Just then Mrs Frost called out and Laura came back to reality with a bump.

'You're in demand,' Antonio said softly. 'If it's something I can help with, I'm just along the corridor.' He smiled and the genuine warmth of it made her feel wretched for ever having doubted him.

CHAPTER EIGHT

MRS FROST'S condition wasn't serious enough to send her to Antonio. Laura guessed she had spent too long napping in the garden and once reassurance and calamine had been dispensed, Mrs Frost left, considerably happier. Not that the elderly lady was alone in her under-estimation of the sun's strength. It was a deceptively overcast May afternoon when a whole family appeared in surgery in varying shades of rose pink.

'We didn't think it was hot enough to get burnt,' the mother said anxiously, telling her son to remove his shirt. 'We walked to the beach from our bed and breakfast and it wasn't until we got settled that I made everyone put on some sunscreen. But I think the worst of it had been done by then. Michael, turn round, love. Show the doctor your back.'

Fourteen-year-old Michael Leigh revealed painful red blisters on his shoulders and a strip of scarlet above his shorts. 'Oh, dear,' Laura sighed. 'That must be uncomfortable, Michael.'

Mrs Leigh offered a glowing neck. 'I got burnt here, even though I was wearing a hat. And my husband's legs are a real mess. Come on, Kev, pull up your trousers.'

Kevin Leigh reluctantly obliged and produced lobster red calves.

'And Janey, too,' Mrs Leigh added, beckoning the little girl with bright pink cheeks. 'We have to leave our accommodation early. Our landlady doesn't like us being there during the day. And there's no where else…inexpensive to go.'

'So you have to stay out all day, irrespective of the

weather?' Laura asked in surprise. Aunt M. had always provided a lounge for visitors, but it seemed that the Leighs hadn't been afforded that courtesy.

'Oh, yes.' Mrs Leigh nodded. 'It's not like a hotel or guest-house—their rules are quite different. But, then, so is the price,' she added fairly.

'So how much of your holiday is left?'

'Another week,' Mr Leigh said. 'Lord knows where we'll go for seven more days.'

'We could go home, I suppose,' Mrs Leigh said doubtfully, but Michael protested.

'Oh, Mum, we can't!'

'But this is my first holiday,' Janey wailed, and Mr Leigh sat down on a chair and lifted her onto his lap.

'Don't cry, pet. Your face is tender enough as it is.'

'Did you say this is your first holiday?' Laura asked, frowning.

'Well, Janey's only six and can't remember the one we had when she was two,' Mrs Leigh replied. 'Since then, we've had a bit of health trouble and haven't gone away.'

'Meg had cancer,' Mr Leigh explained.

Mrs Leigh smiled quickly. 'Yes, but I'm OK now. I had a double mastectomy two years ago.'

'I see,' Laura said with a sympathetic sigh. 'Well, I'll ask the doctor for something to help.' Laura went to Reception where she found Liam Ray, who scribbled out a prescription.

'Corticosteroid to relieve the worst of the symptoms,' Laura told them when she returned. 'And some calamine lotion to help with pain relief. But you must keep out of the sun until healing takes place.'

They were all silent and Meg nodded. 'I think we should go home.'

'But I've had time off school,' Michael complained. 'All for nothing.'

'Well, your father could only get these two weeks off.'

His mother shrugged. 'Come on now, Michael, cheer up. It's not the end of the world.'

Laura admired her spirit. She'd obviously been through hell with her health and this, their first real holiday, seemed doomed.

'Thank you, Nurse Bright,' Meg said, gathering her bags and sliding the prescriptions into her purse. 'Say goodbye, everyone.'

But Janey was in tears and it was then that Laura decided there was one way she could help.

Laura lifted Maria into the shopping cart. 'Just a quick shop, darling,' she whispered, twirling the silky dark curls behind her ear. 'Then we can go home for supper.'

Laura was halfway round the supermarket when Maria squealed. 'Time flies when you're having fun, doesn't it?' a deep voice said beside her.

Laura swivelled around. 'Antonio! What are you doing here?'

'The same as you, by the looks of it.'

Maria wriggled, her tiny hands stretching out. 'Hello, little one. Are you helping Mummy?' He cast a speculative eye over the almost full shopping cart and gave a wry grin. 'You have an empty freezer, I take it?'

Laura laughed, embarrassed. 'Not really. But I think I might have guests soon.'

'At Sea Breeze?' he asked curiously.

She nodded. 'A distressed family. Mother, father and two children.'

'Four? Goodness. Where are you going to put them all?'

She laughed again, her green gaze tangling gently with his. 'I'm just trying to work that out.'

He gave her a wry glance. 'Aha, sounds interesting.'

'They came into the surgery today with sunburn, and they'll have to go home because they're staying in bed and breakfast accommodation. And that means they have to stay out all day and they can't afford to—'

'Hey! Slow down.' He chuckled as Maria tried to wriggle free from her seat. 'You're losing me. Am I allowed to hold her?'

'If you like.' He reached out and took Maria in his arms. 'OK, now tell me as we go.'

Laura found herself explaining about the Leighs as she pushed the cart and he walked beside her. Not that he absorbed much, she was sure, as Maria's little fingers wove playfully in his hair and he laughed, his dark eyes lighting up.

'So that's it, really,' Laura sighed as she balanced the last loaf on the mountain of groceries. 'I just felt so sorry for them. And I do have all that space.'

'Lucky Leighs,' he murmured, sliding her a sexy grin that send her pulse rocketing. 'They found a good Samaritan.'

She stopped at the checkout. 'Well, so did I. Your mother. And, anyway, I won't see much of them. They'll have to fend for themselves mostly.'

He settled Maria in the crook of his arm, one black eyebrow sneaking up. 'And er...all this?' He glanced at the shopping cart.

She laughed as she caught his smile. 'Remember what you said? Hospitality is a way of life in Italy? Well, it is at Sea Breeze, too.'

He nodded slowly as Maria threaded her little arms around his neck and he peered over her shoulder. 'This is nice,' he murmured, and met Laura's anxious gaze. 'But I'm not allowed to say that, am I?'

'I don't seem to be able to stop you.'

He looked at her for an age, then a grin tilted his lips. 'I'm free this evening if you'd like some help. You'll need another bed in that empty room.'

Oh, heavens, Laura thought helplessly, her cheeks flushing as the girl at the checkout waited. After all I've said, I can't weaken now.

Maria snuffled, shamelessly blowing bubbles down her chin and onto Antonio's shirt.

'Now you'll have to say yes,' he said, laughter rumbling up from his chest. 'I've had the official stamp of approval.'

It was a frantic evening. Antonio arrived at seven-thirty after Maria was asleep and they worked side by side in the pretty blue room which he'd started to decorate and she'd finished. She designated it as Mr and Mrs Leigh's and tried to avert her eyes from his jeans-clad legs as he effortlessly heaved two single beds down from upstairs.

He hardly broke a sweat with the mattresses. She noticed a little damp patch on his chest under his light blue T-shirt. And his smooth, muscular biceps bore a sheen that did crazy things to her system. But she managed to pull herself together and spread crisp, clean linen on the beds and hang fresheners in the wardrobe. She added soap and shampoo sachets to the newly cleaned bathroom and placed flowers from the garden in a vase on the window-sill.

At half past nine they considered one of the single rooms, which would be Janey's. 'I could give it a quick coat of emulsion,' Antonio said with a challenging grin. 'Once over with something neutral.'

'I've some downstairs already opened,' Laura said, absently tugging the straps of her pink cotton dungarees back into place.

'What about the boy's room?'

She nodded to the room beside Janey's. 'It just needs a vacuum and fresh linen.'

'OK, we'll go for it, shall we?' He gave her one of those heart-crashing smiles and there was something so casually seductive in it she had to look away. Then she fled, fetching the paint, whilst he brought up ladders and shuffled things around to his liking.

In Michael's room she did her best not to listen to his humming, because that was almost as bad as watching him.

His voice had that deep, echoing resonance that sprang from a hard-muscled frame and broad chest.

'Looks good,' he said later, as he poked his head around her door. 'He'll like it.'

'Do you think so?'

'How old is he?'

'Fourteen. I haven't anything personal for a boy, though,' she said as she sat on the bed. 'I put one of Maria's fluffy animals into Janey's room. It looks a bit bare in here.'

'I might have just the thing,' he said, and she heard him go downstairs and out of the front door. He was back almost immediately.

'Will these do?' He held a pile of magazines in his arms.

'What are they?'

'Cars—flashy, expensive ones that cost the earth.'

She put them on the chest of drawers by the bed. 'Antonio, that's wonderful. Racing cars…sports cars. Where did you get them?'

'Someone gave me them for the surgery. But I think your young lad might appreciate them more. You know, the Leighs are a lucky family,' he went on huskily, leaning against the doorframe, watching her as she arranged them. There was a soft, sensual look to his bone structure that made her feel dizzy, a mobility in his full mouth that made her eyes dance on the smooth curves. Kissable lips, she heard herself thinking, and was shocked that she could think that right now.

They were meant to be working. She wasn't supposed to be standing here, lusting after him. Which was what she was doing. She had no right to think these thoughts. Thoughts of yearning and desire as her eyes took in his body, casually propped against the doorframe, his dark head tilted to one side and his mouth open a fraction.

But such an inviting fraction. She seemed to know in her mind just how he'd taste…and it had nothing to do with the swift kiss he'd given her before. No, she knew exactly what it would be like to be kissed long and hard and passionately. She knew how he'd feel if she touched him and her fingers slid over those arms and broad shoulders.

'They…they deserve some luck,' she managed, dragging her gaze back to the magazines. 'And…and, anyway, there's so much space here. It would be a crime not to use it.'

'Even so,' he said softly in a voice that made her bones melt, 'I can't think of many people who would do what you're doing.'

She gave a little shrug, pushed the magazines firmly into place and tried to hide her shaking hands. What was wrong with her? Why couldn't she control her emotions? She had to get out of the room. Her head was swimming. If she could only make it into the hall…

'Laura?'

'Um…I think I'd better check Maria.' She took a nervous step forward, trying to work out how she'd squeeze through.

'You just did. Five minutes ago. I heard you go downstairs.'

'Yes, but I think I'd better make certain.' She couldn't go forward because Antonio didn't move. And she had nowhere else to go. But with the way he was looking at her, she knew she'd go to pieces if she didn't get out.

'When,' he murmured, swivelling so that his back was against the wall and his hands were thrust into his jeans pockets, 'are you going to trust me?'

She felt as though a snow plough had hit her. A cold shower of goose-bumps ran over her skin as her tummy tightened against the blow. 'That's silly,' she faltered, 'I do trust you.'

'Then why look for escape?'

She laughed nervously. 'I'm not. I was just going—'

'To check on Maria,' he finished for her, his frown disbelieving as he levered himself from the wall and came towards her. 'Yes, I know. But what are you really running from, Laura? What excuse will you use next time?'

'Antonio, it's not fair,' she faltered as his eyes burnt into hers, 'to let you think—'

'I'm a big boy now,' he said softly, his breath fanning her face. 'You won't make me think anything I don't want to. Haven't you noticed? I do have a mind of my own.'

She lifted her eyes, afraid of what she might see. 'I know. And I'm a little afraid of it.'

'Ahh…' he murmured, expelling a long sigh, 'the truth. At last.'

'I can't become involved,' she whispered raggedly. 'It just wouldn't be right. Not for me, or Maria, or for you. And if I were to let you think otherwise—'

'I'm not asking for involvement,' he said in a voice that crackled with emotion. 'Or anything that you don't want to give. The past doesn't equal the future, Laura. And it's not a crime to want to be with someone and share their company.'

She stood where she was, frozen.

He didn't move, but she knew it was only a matter of time. One way or another, this was a confrontation. And he was giving her a choice. And she had to make a decision now. Let him see that she could look into his eyes and still hold on to her traitorously thin shreds of self-control.

'Come here,' he murmured, and he reached out, drawing her towards him. Her sea-green eyes stared up under the golden brown curls that spilled around her face. Her cheeks were on fire, her eyes full of shimmering doubt and her mouth formed into an instinctive O as he inclined his head.

'You are the most beautiful woman I've ever known, Laura,' he said quietly. 'Beautiful inside and out. And I don't know which attracts me the most.'

She didn't know how to respond. Words vanished into thin air. And her eyes were glued to his own brilliantly dark gaze as his fingers trailed sensually down her arms. When they arrived at her wrists, they began to move back up again and she knew she was lost.

Please, let it be over soon, she heard the little voice in her head crying.

No, let it go on for ever, wailed another.

And his fingers trailed up again, over her elbows and the sleeves of her T-shirt and cupped her shoulders. And paused… She couldn't let this happen. She had to let him know that this was just a physical thing. It had nothing to do with what was good for her. Or for him…

'Stop it,' he said quietly, and trickled his hands under her hair and slowly down her back to her waist.

'S-stop what?' she stammered.

'All those waste-of-energy things you're thinking.'

'But…but you don't know what I'm thinking.'

His grin was heart-stopping. 'Oh, yes, I do. I know every thought. I should do. I've made a study of you, Laura Bright. I've watched you every day. Listened to you. And I've kissed you. And now I'm going to kiss you again. But this time…I want you to kiss me back. And remember, a kiss has to prove one thing.'

'One…thing…?'

'Yes, simply that both people want to do it again.'

'What if…if they don't want to…to kiss again?' Silly question. Her body was in uproar at his touch and only a fool would have thought otherwise.

'Then they don't,' he whispered reasonably. 'It's over. Done with.'

'Finished?'

'Oh, yes, quite finished.'

She stared at him, every cell in her body quivering as his hand came up to cup her chin and she waited as something far more powerful than the snow-plough effect happened. Simply, she forgot everything. All that she'd tried to say, to explain, all the reasons why it wasn't good to be doing this and be enjoying it so much. It was a kiss that she couldn't describe and as many times afterwards as she tried to put it into context she couldn't.

Cosmic, Shelley would have said. Out of this world. And

it was. A kiss that was pure pleasure and pain and bitter-sweet need, exposing the emptiness inside her. It was so intense and incredible that all the lonely places that ached for comfort inside her were filled. And as they were filled, Laura knew that the second Antonio's mouth had covered hers, she'd wanted more.

As his lips raked hungrily over hers, she responded with a hunger that shocked her. His tongue tangled with hers and the pressure of his mouth made her gasp as he took her mouth again, claiming it for his own. For all her fine words, she needed him. Wanted him more than she had ever wanted anyone. Including Mark. But how could she? How could she want this man so much when she'd thought she'd loved Mark?

'Oh, Laura,' he grated as he lifted his mouth and stared down at her kiss-bruised lips. 'Laura, what are you doing to me?'

She knew what she was doing. She was giving him his proof. She wanted to kiss him again. What had happened to the Laura who had protested so much? Now she wanted the whole of this man, heart and soul.

She ached for his touch and as if in answer to her thoughts his hand came up to slip the cotton strap from her shoulder, his fingers easing it slowly down, leaving only the light fabric of her T-shirt between his fingers and her flesh. Then they slipped slowly over the hard, aching peak of one breast. His eyes flashed wider for a moment and she was ashamed of her transparent desire. Her body was flying in the face of her words and he knew it.

Slowly he traced a circle and cupped the soft mound with his palm, a groan escaping his lips. 'Oh, Laura,' he whispered, the lids of his eyes drooping so sexily that her heart almost stood still.

And he kissed her again, his fingers tearing through her hair and scorching her scalp and then returning to the swelling curves under her T-shirt. And there was nothing she could do as his hand slipped under the cotton and up to her breast, his fingers sliding experimentally over the lace.

His fingers were deft and sure and found their way over the delicate edge of the bra as their kiss threatened to burn out of control. His lips were hot and passionate and they stumbled back against the wall, where for one heart-pounding moment he cradled her, their breathing hard and fast.

She saw the desire in his eyes and knew that nothing could stop this now. That her need was as great as his, if not greater. Then his hand came up to her shoulder, taking the other strap which had somehow miraculously remained in place. He lifted it, one brow arching slightly as if in question before he began to draw it down.

As he did so, something in the house stirred. Like a sigh of a breeze, a cool flutter of evening air. But it had the effect of stilling his hand and for a few precious moments she held her breath as they listened to the silence around them.

'Laura…' Antonio whispered. He shook his head a little, then lifted himself. The heat of their bodies cooled fractionally and instead of sliding her strap down, he slowly drew up the fallen one. Tenderly he lifted her chin and gazed into her eyes.

'You're afraid,' he said so softly she could barely hear. 'And I can't bear that.'

Had she been afraid? she wondered, still numbed. Had he seen fear in her eyes? All she had known was that for a few minutes she had been on another planet. And if that was scary, then, yes, perhaps so.

He took her wrist, his breath coming shallowly, and led her out of the room and downstairs. Her legs were so shaky she almost missed her footing, but he saw and lifted her gently down the last two steps, encircling her in his arms at the bottom.

'Let's sit for a while,' he said, and she nodded. They looked in on Maria and she was sleeping so they went into the little lounge and opened the long windows onto the garden. It was a beautiful night, with a sky studded with stars. Scents off the sea washed over them and, without switching on the light, they sat on the sofa, holding hands.

'Come here,' he whispered, and she leaned into him, her heart skittering wildly in her chest as he threaded an arm around her and held her close.

'Talk to me,' he whispered. 'Tell me what you want.'

She felt his fingers around hers, probing the sides of her thumbs and running softly across her palms. There was no urgency in them as before. Just a gentle invitation and a closeness that made her heart ache. 'I thought I knew what I wanted,' she said, leaning her head on his shoulder. 'I had it all worked out. Sell Sea Breeze. Go back to London. Find us a home. And live my life.'

'Alone?' His voice was hushed, a little shaky. 'Always and for ever alone?'

'I hadn't thought that far. I couldn't. Not after Mark.'

His chest lifted. 'Are you in love with him?'

She hadn't expected that question and it surprised her. She hadn't even asked herself if she still loved Maria's father. How could she love a man who had abandoned her? How could she love someone who had treated his little daughter and his secret family so badly? Had she ever loved him or had it been something else that she hadn't been able to define until now?

'Don't answer,' Antonio said then. 'I shouldn't have asked.'

'It's just that—' she began, but he turned and cupped her face with his hands.

'I'm rushing you,' he said quietly. 'I knew that the moment I kissed you.'

She shook her head fiercely. 'But I wanted to kiss you back.'

In the darkness he smiled. 'Then there's hope for me yet.'

It was a long, lingering moment and neither of them spoke until slowly he disentangled himself.

'Is there anything else you need me to do for tomorrow?'

'No,' she murmured, swallowing.

'Then good luck with your family.'

'Are you leaving?' she asked forlornly.

'I think I must, don't you?'

She nodded and he bent, softly touching her face with the tips of his fingers and brushing a kiss on her cheek. 'Goodnight, *caro*,' he whispered.

Her heart missed a beat as he stood up and reached out to grasp her hands and bring her to her feet. There in the little darkened room, with the scents of the sea blowing in and mixing with the subtle fragrance of lemons, they said goodnight. She walked with him to the front door and watched him go, his broad shoulders hunched as he unlocked his vehicle, climbed in and closed the door.

Laura lingered to see the taillights disappear, leaning back against the wall, hugging her arms around her waist. What had happened this evening? Had she been afraid? Yes. But not of Antonio.

Of herself.

Of the depth of emotion inside her. Of how much she had wanted him. If he hadn't stopped when he had, would she have found the strength to?

Too tired now to find an answer, she closed the door and went to check Maria. Her small face was nestled on the pillow and Laura bent and kissed her forehead and crept out.

Then she went upstairs to the room where Antonio had been working. He had drawn away the protective covers and piled them neatly in a corner. The walls looked fresh and light and the room smelt of emulsion and his cologne. She sat on the bed and inhaled it, her fingers going up to her lips, tracing their fullness. They quivered on a sigh as she remembered what she had done and shamelessly wondered if she would ever do it again.

CHAPTER NINE

THE Leighs arrived the following morning and were delighted with their rooms. 'We'll never be able to thank you enough,' Meg said gratefully as oohs and ahhs echoed from Janey's and Michael's rooms.

'I'm a dab hand with the mower,' Kevin Leigh told her. 'And your grass needs cutting. It's a shady garden so I won't be in the sun.'

'That would be great.' Laura smiled. 'And if you want to use the garden furniture, it's still in the shed. It'll be somewhere for you all to sit other than your rooms.'

Just then the phone rang and Laura hurried down to answer it. The estate agents wanted to view Sea Breeze that afternoon and she arranged a time, suddenly realizing how helpful having the Leighs would be. The place was up and running—complete with guests!

On Monday, Antonio met her in the hall just after surgery. His sleek black hair was a little longer now, giving him a rakish look, and his dark eyes were trained on her as they met halfway. 'Your family moved in?' he asked, as a cool drift of lemon engulfed her.

'Mmm. And they loved their rooms.'

'For a last-minute rush,' he said, quirking an eyebrow, 'we did pretty well.' As he spoke, a woman appeared from the waiting room. He stiffened, casting her a smile as she approached. Laura noted her slight flush as Antonio spoke a few words of greeting.

She wondered if he had the same effect on most women and her thoughts flew to Mark who had turned so many heads in his quiet way.

She watched Antonio talking to the woman and wondered about the dark-haired girl. The image was still clear in her mind—a beautiful young woman with long black hair and classical features that no man would forget in a hurry.

What did she really know about this man? Only what was on the surface. What he wanted her to see and know. Michelle's and Becky's remarks had influenced her, no doubt. But if his past was littered with females, there was no reason for him to disclose it. And why should it make a difference anyway? A man of thirty-four had to have a history—and there was no doubt of his sex appeal. She was still trying to resist it, even though what had happened on Friday night had sent her heart tumbling around her feet.

'Laura?'

'Oh—sorry. What?'

The woman had gone and he was frowning at her. 'I had Louise Graham in early this morning. Her husband came, too. Bethany's decided against a termination. They aren't happy people, but their daughter seems to have made up her mind. Ravi referred her to an obstetrician and she'll come to the clinic for antenatals.'

Laura nodded slowly. 'And the baby?'

He gave a little frown. 'Adoption, probably.' His fingers came up to brush her cheek. 'Laura, would you and Maria come to Canzone again? Say…the weekend?'

She felt her heart pound. How could she refuse? He was a sexy, gorgeous guy and, damn it, she wanted to be with him, more than anything else in the world. So she agreed and spent the rest of the afternoon cursing herself for it.

On Wednesday, Bethany made a shy appearance at the antenatal clinic. Mo Fielding was busy with the newest pregnancies and Becky was seeing routine cases, so Laura took Bethany aside into the little room in which they'd talked before. It was just two o'clock and Bethany said she'd had a free period and so had come straight from school in her uniform.

'I might...' Bethany hesitated as they sat down '...have the baby adopted.'

'There's a lot to consider,' Laura acknowledged. 'Would you like to know about our screening procedures?'

Bethany nodded. 'I'm really nervous.'

'Don't be. You've already had some of your blood and urine tests and your first scan is on Friday.' Laura glanced at the notes in front of her. 'This first one is carried out to date your pregnancy accurately and to detect any abnormalities.'

'Abnormalities? The baby will be all right, won't it?' Bethany looked alarmed.

'Scans are routine, Bethany. We check regularly to make certain the baby is healthy. Sometimes more are recommended to check your baby's growth and the location of the placenta and the amount of amniotic fluid—the substance that surrounds the foetus in the uterus.'

'Why do you have to have blood tests all the time?'

'The blood and urine tests reveal a great deal,' Laura explained. 'We discover your blood group and check for things like anaemia, hepatitis B and anything that might be helpful to know about as far as your health is concerned as the baby develops.'

'Will I be able to see the baby inside me?'

Laura nodded. 'Oh, yes. We check on the foetal heartbeat by electronic monitoring.'

'Is that painful?'

'Not at all. It's a very straightforward and simple procedure.'

'How many times do I have to come to the clinic?' Bethany asked with a frown.

'If all goes well, we see you every month until the twenty-eighth week, then every two weeks until the thirty-sixth. Then weekly until your delivery date.'

'So how long is a pregnancy?' Bethany asked, running a hand over her stomach.

'On average, forty weeks from the first day of your last period.'

'It's a lot to think about. I never imagined all this when Tony—' She stopped, going scarlet. 'Oh, heavens, I didn't mean to say his name. You won't tell anyone, will you?'

'Not if you don't want me to. But can you really go through this alone?'

Bethany sniffed. 'I'll have to. He's only sixteen. And he's got exams, too.'

But Laura couldn't help thinking that sooner or later Bethany would need Tony's support in the crucial decisions she would have to make.

The Leighs had a great week, adopting the shady garden as their retreat. They took walks out over the cliffs and went shopping and ate at Molly's café. Mr Leigh mowed the grass and erected Aunt M.'s forgotten garden furniture. Laura almost cried with joy when she saw it all.

The family left for their last shopping expedition on the following Saturday and Laura drove to Canzone. It was a scintillating June morning, one of those days when the sea was a saucer of liquid silver and mischievous breezes blew over the water.

Maria squealed in recognition of the house as Laura nudged the car through the gate. She felt like a schoolgirl on a first date. Her heart was pounding ridiculously fast. Another squeal brought Laura's head round fast.

Antonio was walking from the house, his long, tanned legs striding out under his shorts. His smile left all smiles standing. Wide, full lips parted to reveal glistening white teeth that had no right to be so perfect when every other feature was just as perfect.

His eyes were somewhere between plain chocolate and jet. If she had to make a stab at it, jet would win. Long black lashes fanned down on smooth tanned skin. Heavy, lazy lids lay across the dark pupils, as though he'd just climbed out of bed.

Bed...

A flush went over her. Laura swallowed.

She was trying to handle her emotions. Trying to steady her nerves. To think of ice-cold showers. Long bracing walks. Jogging in the rain. None of which helped as he bent to open the car door, the deep blue T-shirt straining across the width of his chest.

Laura climbed out of the car, relieved that she'd also chosen to wear shorts and nothing more formal. His eyes reflected his approval as they skimmed over her long, lightly tanned legs and upward to the strappy white cotton top. It exposed a tiny inch of bare midriff and she felt suddenly self-conscious as his eyes dragged almost unwillingly to her face.

Nervously, she tucked little tendrils of hair into her peaked cap. His gaze flickered on the smooth creamy arch of her neck. And stayed there. Until she was forced to reach into the car for Maria, unable to bear the suspense.

But he caught her wrist and slowly pulled her towards him. Then he inclined his head under the peak of her cap and looked into her eyes. 'Good morning, *caro*,' he whispered huskily.

'G-good morning,' she breathed as he bent, kissing each cheek very slowly in a Continental-style greeting. His lips hovered as she stared up into his eyes, unable to move.

'You look gorgeous. A perfect start,' he murmured, pressuring her wrist gently, 'to a perfect day.'

The next thing she knew he was reaching for Maria, his long, supple body exuding a wave of delicious lemon. Ashamed of her thoughts, Laura hurried to the boot and opened it. But she looked at its contents blindly, terrified at the incredible craving inside her.

He had been so close. His lips had lingered long enough to make her skin burn. As she stared into the boot, her hand went up to touch her cheek. The smooth scrape of his beard had glanced across it. Everything that was masculine and powerful had been embodied in that greeting. It had almost knocked her off balance.

And with a superhuman effort at self-control, she lifted out her holdall, grateful for a few precious moments in which to recover.

After stowing away her bag in the little study in which she'd talked to Elena Dallori, they left for the sea. They walked for miles, enjoying the wild, whippy breeze and the spine-tingling smells from the ocean. Finally Antonio turned the buggy down a path that led to the sea.

Two green wings of cliffside marked their descent. Antonio guided the buggy, his large hands controlling it easily as he shifted over the pebbled terrain. When they reached the sand, a wide and stunning expanse of white beach gave way to a rolling sea. The blue-green water was undisturbed by swimmers and Laura could only see one other couple in the distance.

'It's beautiful here,' Laura said, aware of the warm sun caressing them and thankful she had rubbed in plenty of sunscreen. Maria was well covered, too, and under her little sun canopy she was well protected.

'Yes, it is. Much the same as Capri,' he murmured softly. 'Which is why *Mamma* came down here every day. It reminded her of home. Let's rest over there,' he suggested, pointing over her shoulder. 'We'll have the shade of the cliff and the rocks to sit on.'

'Don't you ever miss Italy?' Laura asked, as he turned the buggy in one easy movement and pulled it over the sand behind him. They ambled to a tiny island of red-brown rocks and he guided the buggy in between, shielding it from the rays of the sun.

'I had Canzone del Mare built so that I wouldn't get homesick.' He shrugged as Laura clambered onto one of the flatter rocks and lifted her legs, positioning her feet for balance. 'Canzone, as you know, is a replica of our house in Capri. This beach reminds me of a place close by. It's called Marina Piccola.'

'That's a lovely name,' Laura murmured. 'Tell me what it's like.'

His eyes met hers with a dark intensity. 'Breathtaking. Colours that deepen as the day goes on. Sunsets that burn like fire. The sea is endless and warm and amazingly blue. And there's a rock there…' His long, tanned fingers smoothed absently over the hard, sculptured stone he was sitting on. 'We call her Lo Scoglio delle Sirene.' He smiled softly as she frowned. 'Mermaid's Rock.'

Laura sighed. 'That's beautiful.'

'So you see, I have found little Italy here…' he glanced over the turquoise waters '…and built my home above it. I have the best of both worlds.'

His soft, husky voice made her shiver as he stretched out, his long, athletic body taking up at least three rocks. He was so virile and sensual and every move took her breath away as one arm trailed down to rock the buggy.

Laura saw Maria's little eyes close as he rocked it. Did he do that naturally? she wondered, adjusting her sunglasses. She felt safe behind them. He couldn't look into her eyes and see her soul. What she was thinking. And what was in her heart.

He seemed so natural with Maria. He looked as though he pushed a buggy every day. It was very confusing and Laura had to focus her mind as he spoke about Italy.

But it wasn't long before he turned the conversation around to her again. 'And you, Laura? What do *you* want?' he asked as he raised himself from the rock. His long legs were stretched out, his strong, curved ankles crossed casually, the powerful arch of one foot drawing her eyes upward along the giddy lines of his long legs.

He looked sculptured, too, she realized with a little jolt. Just like the rocks he was sitting on. As though every muscle and joint had been created out of some master plan and had ended in perfection.

Laura could see dustings of black hair sprinkled over his calves, continuing above his knee and disappearing beneath the hem of his shorts. Then again at his throat, clamouring to be free from the restriction of his T-shirt. They looked so fine and silky, as superbly exotic as his dark, grainy skin. The firm muscle of his forearms protruded as he folded his arms thoughtfully, his dark head inclined.

'I told you before,' she replied uncertainly, hardly able to meet his eyes. Her hand was resting on the peak of her cap, her body tense. 'I know it sounds boring—'

'No, it doesn't. Nothing you've told me has been boring.'

Suddenly she had the urge to remove her cap and her sunglasses, let down her hair and allow him to look into her eyes. But she resisted, knowing she was too vulnerable to those piercing dark pools of liquid jet that were assessing her carefully.

'Everything I do,' she tried haltingly, 'is for Maria. You know that.'

'I know.' He nodded slowly, one brow tucking up in a question mark. 'But at twenty-six, you have your life ahead of you—'

'I have *our* life ahead of me,' she corrected gently.

'And you'd sacrifice happiness for security?' His eyes momentarily flashed.

'Don't you think the two can go together?'

He gave her a dry little smile. 'Perhaps so.'

The slight tilt of his head and his soft voice made her heart fly like a trapped bird and she tried to gather her scattered senses. The sound of the sea washed over them like a caressing wave and the air around them felt charged. The lurching movement of her stomach made her wonder what kind of spell he had over her. Whatever it was, it seemed to gather momentum and she felt so close to him that she wanted to reach out and touch him.

But of course she didn't, and as Maria stirred in her pram she lowered her eyes. 'I think it's time we made our way back,' she said, and slid down from the rock. Antonio gave her a long, thoughtful look as his eyes tried to penetrate the sunglasses. But then he raised himself from the rocks and reached to ease out the buggy. Together they walked back across the sand and the tension between them eased as they climbed up the cliff path. By the time they reached Antonio's home they had found safer topics of conversation and they talked easily.

Like friends.

Like friends who were just walking, not wanting more than the moment. And each other's company.

But when they arrived back at Canzone and entered the cool, modern kitchen, the little red light beside the phone was blinking. He lifted it and began to speak and Laura pushed the buggy into the hall to allow him privacy.

As she lifted Maria into her arms, she heard his tone soften as he spoke a woman's name. Her heart raced and she climbed the stairs and went up into the little study where she'd left her bag.

Ten minutes later he joined her, his expression unreadable as he suggested they have lunch on the terrace. He made no mention of the call and Laura couldn't help wondering if her visit to Canzone had been a dreadful mistake.

CHAPTER TEN

AFTER lunch, they sat in the garden on steamer chairs and talked endlessly until finally Maria yawned, snuggling into the cushions.

'Little sleepyhead,' Antonio murmured affectionately.

'Perhaps we should go.'

He looked surprised. 'But why? She can nap in the family room.'

But Laura felt uneasy. She wasn't sure she wanted to be alone with him. Not with the way she was feeling, so mellow and content and utterly at peace in the flower-filled garden. But he slid her an easy smile and she found herself walking with him into the house. He took them upstairs to the family room and she laid Maria on the changing mat. He left her to it and afterwards she settled Maria in the cot. Her little daughter needed no coaxing and she curled on her side, her thumb wedged in her mouth.

Laura went downstairs and found Antonio in the little office. He was sitting at a workstation and papers spilled over it, the breeze blowing in through the window.

His dark head was bent, his broad shoulders strained against the cloth of his T-shirt. Thick, black hair kissed his collar and looked so tempting. She wanted to touch it, to see if it felt as good as it looked.

Suddenly he looked round. 'Is she asleep?'

'Mmm. Totally bushed.' She peered over his shoulder at the papers. 'Would this be "Hands? Our Key Diagnostic Tool"?'

A dark brow arched. 'Very good.'

'I'm curious,' she murmured, propping her head against

the doorjamb and folding her arms. 'Why hands and not, say, feet? Or ears?'

He turned the swivel chair fully, stretching out his long, bare legs and making her wish she wasn't in such close proximity.

'Consider this,' he murmured, licking his full lips thoughtfully, which did nothing to ease the commotion inside her. 'On a yearly average, twenty per cent of A and E patients need their hands fixing.'

She looked impressed. 'As high as that.'

'Surprising, isn't it? We patch this complex machinery up and hope for the best. But we don't really understand the logistics or long-term consequences of, say, infection or bad fractures.' He raised his eyebrows questioningly. 'Shall I go on?'

Laura smiled. 'Please, do.'

'Take one bad infection. The right antibiotic. And time. But what happens when we get it wrong? The infection spreads like wildfire. Moves through tendons and tissue like lightning. The system crashes and so does the patient.' He shrugged. 'All because we took an insignificant injury for granted or didn't have time to investigate a difficult one.'

She nodded slowly. 'You're right. We see a lot of hand injuries at the surgery. Sometimes wounds and fractures take months to clear. And children especially are always so low after antibiotic.'

'My point exactly.'

'So you're saying we could do better?'

'Much. Given funding and research.' He stood then, unravelling his long, powerful limbs, and came towards her, unlatching her wrists from her waist and lifting her hands, turning them palms upwards. 'Hands…' he murmured, trailing a long, tanned finger with a short well-trimmed nail across her palm. She held her breath, fighting the urge to let out a sigh. 'They are not only beautiful but a mine of medical information.' He gave her palms a soft brush with his fingertips, causing every nerve in her body to jolt. 'The colour and size and fingers tell us so much.'

It was all she could do to avoid the pull of his eyes as his fingers worked a sensual path across her hands. He spread out her fingers, trailing his thumb over them so slowly that she wanted to scream. 'Such beautiful nails,' he breathed, smoothing the soft skin around them.

If she hadn't looked up then…but she did. Her green eyes locked with his and an aching, traitorous wave of desire shot through her. A dark flush filled his face until finally he released her hands and she let them fall to her sides, pressing them against her thighs as though her palms had been burnt.

'Coffee, I think,' he said a little harshly, and she nodded turning to walk to the room ahead, her heart making a frantic attempt to escape from the cage of her chest.

Laura sat in the luxurious white-walled room with picture windows overlooking the sea. From the half-moon rattan sofa with its thick creamy pillows, she gazed out across the ocean. It was a view not dissimilar to the dining room at Sea Breeze. An uninterrupted blue slash of the sea and a cloudless sky.

The blinds outside shielded the room from the glare of the sun and the stillness was perfect, save for the soft chirping of the birds. If only she could regain her composure before he returned with coffee…

Laura forced her mind to focus on the character of the room and not on the whirl of confused emotions inside her. She didn't want to think of what had happened just now. Neither did she want to think about the phone call earlier that he had so discreetly avoided mentioning.

The room was very Italian. Little raffia mats adorned the shelves, as did pottery and clay figurines that were hand-painted in bright colours. Large terracotta pots stood on the pale floor tiles and were filled with blooms. The room was a reflection of Antonio and she wondered how many women had sat here, thinking the same thing.

He came in with a tray of coffee and biscuits and lowered it to the simple wooden coffee-table. She wished she had brought a skirt to change into. Sitting in this elegant room in shorts and a skimpy little top didn't seem very appropriate somehow.

He poured dark, rich coffee into chunky, solid cups. 'Cream?' he asked, but she declined and he passed her a cup which she sipped thoughtfully.

'What are you thinking?' He sat beside her, the inches dwindling between them.

'I was admiring this room,' she began, but he shook his head slowly.

'Tell me the truth, Laura.'

'That was the truth.'

'Not the whole of it.'

She blushed and he took her half-filled cup and lowered it to the coffee-table. Then he sat back, closer this time, and ran an arm along the top of the sofa behind her head.

'Were you thinking of Maria's father?'

Laura looked at him in surprise. 'No. What makes you ask that?'

He wrinkled his brow. 'You had a far-away look in your eyes.'

'I was thinking about Italy,' she said with a hesitant smile. 'Sitting here like this and looking out over the sea, I felt I could almost be there.'

He nodded slowly, his eyes searing over her. Suddenly she felt his fingers in her hair, twisting the strands lightly. 'Capri is very beautiful.'

Her eyes went up to his. They were such beautiful eyes, earth-brown flecks distilling the almost ebony irises, which was why she could never quite tell if they were black or dark brown. Their heavy, sensual lids made him look so Italian and she inhaled unsteadily, sensing their power.

She knew he was feeling something powerful, too. So

powerful he was trying to fight it as his fingers stilled in her hair. And for a moment they sat perfectly still, the silence unbearable.

'Laura, you know what is happening to us, don't you?'

She knew. She had known for weeks. Maybe from the first day she had met him.

'Don't be frightened,' he whispered. 'Have faith in me.'

The words touched her soul. All her senses strained towards Antonio. She could feel vibrant, masculine waves coming off his body and sucking in her own vibrations. Every breath she breathed was an effort. His hand slipped to her shoulder, his fingers running over her bare skin.

'I want to kiss you, Laura. Properly,' he breathed on a shaken whisper, his lips so close she could almost taste them. 'And you want that, too. I know it.'

She had wanted it for such a long time. Dreamed of it. She needed to know what it was like to taste him. She needed to satisfy the craving in her soul that wouldn't go away.

His hand moved down her arm and drew her to him whilst the other came across to clasp her. He pressed her close and her mouth opened on a soft gasp.

'I *know*,' he muttered, 'that you feel it, too. This connection…this link.'

His voice was like waves washing over her body. She was trying to hold onto what little reality she had left. Trying to remember all the reasons why she shouldn't be doing this. Even the thought of Maria asleep upstairs couldn't stop her. Her body and mind were beyond control as he bent his head and took her mouth in a kiss that was so devastating she felt her whole system surrender.

His lips were relentless, demanding her true response. And she gave it, her arms snaking around his neck, her breasts pressed hard against his chest. Closing her eyes, she gave herself up to him.

Their kiss was fire itself, lighting her up with a warmth that was nothing to do with external heat. It was a fire kindled by their passion and desire. Her fingers drew down his head, his beautiful thick, black hair slipping wildly through her fingers.

His tongue explored her mouth and the touch of his fingers on her skin made her senses reel. His fingers deftly linked around the thin strap of her top and slipped it over her shoulder. Softly he whispered words in his native language which she couldn't comprehend. Sexy, delicious words spoken with raspy breath that fanned over her face and neck. Words that felt like exquisite oil trailing over her skin and into her mind, weaving some kind of unbelievable magic.

There was a message in them that woke up all her emotions, even though she didn't know their true meaning. She'd never realized what a powerful tool language could be when its meaning had to be guessed at.

His hand found the swell of her breast and a sigh caught in her throat as her fingers curved and scraped against his neck.

Their eyes met, briefly, then he took her mouth in a kiss of flames.

How long, she wondered, could she bear the onslaught? Blood pulsed through her ears and up to her temples and her breath stilled in her chest as his hand found the naked expanse of skin at her waist. His body stiffened, tensed and he pulled her against him with a groan of desire.

'*Mi amore*,' he whispered, and his hand travelled up to the lacy curves of her bra. He cupped one full, throbbing mound beneath, claiming the aching bud that was so shamelessly needy for his touch.

Her hand went up, curving under his T-shirt. Hard, sleek muscle rippled beneath her touch and heat flared from the curve of his backbone and broad shoulders. Blindly she began to sink into that other world, wanting him as part of her.

Then a cold little shiver went down her neck. What was she thinking? What was she doing? A terrified little voice was screaming in her head. Remember, this had happened before and disaster had struck soon afterwards. Her emotions were running away with her, drugging her. She pushed away and opened her eyes.

'What is it?' he asked raggedly. His face was flushed and his eyes heavy. What had she done? Why had she led him on when she had no intention of sleeping with him?

It couldn't happen. No matter how much her body craved him, there was no way she would allow herself to go down that road. A repetition of the past. Failure to realize that it was just sexual attraction and nothing more.

After Maria's birth, her world had changed. Maria came first in everything. And nothing on earth would threaten that. She had believed Mark. Believed every word he had said. That they would marry and have a family. Be as other couples were. Spend the rest of their lives together. And when he had assured her of this, she had given way. Compromised her values and belief system. The result of which was her darling child, who would never know the love of her biological father.

'I...I'm sorry, Antonio,' she stammered, prising herself away, but he held her still, forcing her to look into his eyes.

'There is no reason to be sorry. I want what you want, *caro*. And this is not the time.' He slowly released her, lifting a hand to drape a lock of her hair behind her ear.

'Laura, I will never do anything to hurt you,' he murmured in a deep voice that shook a little as he sat back. His hand ground into his hair, the thick black strands falling through his fingers as he thrust them over his head.

Could she believe him? she wondered, keeping her body stiff and on the defensive. It wasn't his fault that she had let him think they could make love. But she had to make it clear now. 'Antonio, I didn't mean this to happen,' she said firmly, her voice under control now.

'And you stopped us,' he agreed without hesitation. 'You have great strength.' He smiled softly, his broad chest lifting on a sigh. 'The moment ran away with us. I'm only human, *caro*. And you are a very beautiful woman.'

And you, Antonio Dallori, she thought achingly, are the most beautiful man I have ever met.

And dangerous. *So* dangerous.

'Shall we go up to your little daughter?' he asked, and she nodded.

He reached for her hand and drew her to her feet. 'Don't let this afternoon trouble you,' he assured her, cupping her face in his hands. 'We are…still friends, you and I?'

She felt her heart flutter, knowing that friendship, for her, was only half of the equation. 'Friends,' she said.

He searched her eyes, then nodded and they went up to Maria, who opened her eyes sleepily. Laura lifted her, grateful for her warm little body to hug.

Their parting was brief and the last brush of his lips on her cheek was still tingling on her skin as she drove away from Canzone. And when she got home, somehow she managed to greet the Leighs with a smile and sit in the garden with them for the rest of the evening.

She was grateful for the distraction. Grateful that she was in company because if she'd been left to herself she would have mentally replayed the whole day over and over. And the gnawing inside her would have deepened and she wouldn't have trusted herself not to phone…to think up some excuse just to hear his voice again.

The Leighs left on Sunday and Sea Breeze was empty again. Laura rattled around in it for the next two weeks, wondering if any of the people the estate agent had showed round were interested. June accelerated into July and Laura saw less of Antonio. Ravi Chandra and Liam Ray had holidays booked and a locum arrived.

He was competent and thorough, but slow. Antonio patiently spent time with him, but it set him back with his own lists.

'Too many temporary residents today,' Sally Granger,

one of the reception staff told Laura one Friday morning. 'Could you manage a couple more? I've got one with a burn from a camping stove and a BP.'

Laura nodded and was about to leave when a man ran in, his T-shirt covered in blood. 'Help!' he yelled, waving his bandaged hand as blood oozed down his wrist. 'I sawed through my fingers!'

The blood seemed to be seeping from under the cloth and there was a towel tied tightly round his upper arm. She managed to get him to her room, uncertain where he'd been cut. 'Sit down,' she told him. She wrestled off the tourniquet and raised the blood-soaked limb above his head.

Blood spurted from a triple gash across the inside of his fingers. She plugged it with a sterile pad and used several more to staunch the flow. Slowly, colour came back to his face. He swallowed, staring up in surprise.

'Is…is it stopping?'

She nodded as she applied pressure. 'How did you do it?'

'A mechanical saw. Working on pipes… Lost concentration for a bit. I thought I'd sawed off my fingers. Are they still there?'

'They're there.' She grinned. 'Who tied the tourniquet?'

'My mate. He said it'd stop the bleeding.'

'It doesn't.' She shrugged. 'It unfortunately just makes things worse. That's why you were bleeding so much. You've two big arches of arteries called arcades in your hand. They go through the palm and into the fingers. The blood supply is really rich—like striking oil. So we need to elevate your hand immediately. Why didn't they call an ambulance?'

'Because I knew there was a surgery here. I was working on the building across the road from you. I thought I could save time.'

Just then Antonio appeared in the doorway. His face fell. 'Lord, what happened here?'

She told him what had happened and he rolled his eyes.

'You're lucky,' he told their patient as Laura carefully applied fresh pads. 'But you'll need attention.'

'You can't sew me up?'

'I could. But you'd curse me in a couple of months if you couldn't use that hand properly. They need to check out the tendons at the hospital.'

After he'd done what he could, he called an ambulance and packed the man off to hospital.

'Will he be OK?' Laura asked as they stood in her room.

He offered a tired little smile. 'Let's hope he's one of the twenty per cent who are referred for treatment.' He thrust his hand wearily through his hair. 'I was called out last night—just a gastric upset. On my way back, there was an accident. I went to see if I could help, but it was a head-on collision. Both drivers had been killed. One of the cars was recognizable—just.' He looked down at his hands, rubbing his thumb distractedly. 'It was Mitchell Fraser's.'

'Oh, no...' Laura closed her eyes.

'The police suspect alcohol.' He gave a growl of frustration. 'I should have seen this coming. I should have found a way to make him see sense.'

'But you tried,' she protested. 'You saved his life once.'

'It wasn't enough.'

'What more could you have done?'

'I don't know. But I should have found a way.'

'He had a second chance, Antonio,' she reminded him gently. 'A chance that you gave him. He just needed to take it.'

It was all she could say. It was all she could do. And he drew her into his arms and rested his chin against her head, a shuddering sigh going through him as she held him close.

CHAPTER ELEVEN

ANTONIO needed her, quite desperately, but finally he mustered control, prising Laura away with gentle firmness. 'Thank you,' he muttered, and plastered on a smile. 'Sorry to hold you up.'

'It's nothing,' she replied, feeling awkward. 'You're… OK?'

'I'm fine.'

She knew he wasn't. He stood there, one hand running through his hair, his dark eyes shielded, looking lost and alone.

'Are you busy this evening?' she found herself asking.

'No…not really. Why?'

Her eyes were level with his. And she saw astonishment in his gaze as she asked if he'd like to have supper with her. Not just surprise, she realized afterwards, but yearning, desire, confusion. All the things that had frightened her before and now were blown away.

'Laura…I can't.' His mouth worked a little and he shook his head helplessly. 'It's not that I don't want to. I do. Very much.' He lifted his eyes to the ceiling and let them drop heavily. 'Oh, hell, *caro*. What I'm trying to say is, I can't guarantee—'

'I know,' she broke in softly. 'I know you can't. But the invitation is still there.'

He looked shaken and amazed and then walked slowly back towards her. 'Do you mean it?'

She nodded and lifted her face. He bent his head and kissed her hair and brushed it back from her face with his hands. 'Don't pity me, Laura. Don't do *this* out of pity.'

It wasn't pity. Not even close. Something inside her had

melted today. Some part of her soul that was nothing to do with the past, or Mark, but with her and what she alone wanted. She suddenly realized how important the moment had been. If she was to go the rest of her life without loving, real loving, then today would always be there to remind her there was love. True love. For she'd known as she'd held him that she was in love with him. The bitterness and disappointment Mark had instilled in her had evaporated.

Stubble grazed her cheeks and she inhaled a musky scent as he whispered, 'I'll be there.'

Laura had the rest of the day to get through and it wasn't easy. She saw her two extras and another two after lunch—wound dressings and a tetanus. But as Becky was off she worked right up until four and it was only on her way to the crèche that she allowed herself to think about what she had done.

Would Antonio come tonight? What must he think? After all she had said.

Was she thinking rationally? Was she out of her mind?

Then she glanced in her rear-view mirror and all her questions were answered. Deep green pools of desire gazed back at her, alive and vibrant. She wanted Antonio. Needed him. And she knew that he wanted her.

Laura stopped at the chemist before collecting Maria. It was a call that made her legs shake a little because she hadn't needed to think about contraception before. But she couldn't ignore or shelve the possibility, even though she'd feel a fool if he didn't arrive.

Antonio arrived at seven, his white shirt crumpled a little and his tie slightly undone. There was a dark, rakish growth on his face as he stared at her from under hooded eyes. He said nothing and neither did Laura as she let him in, but as soon as the door was closed he pulled her into his arms. 'Are you sure you want me here?' His voice was ragged and husky and she slid her arms around his neck, bringing down his head close to her face.

'Does this tell you?'

He nodded, growling under his breath. 'Why, *caro*? Why now—tonight?'

She shuddered in his arms in her thin cotton dress and his hands smoothed over it needfully. 'Because of us…just us…' She lifted her eyes. 'I stopped thinking ahead—or backwards today. After Mitchell Fraser, it just seemed important…to live for the moment.' Her voice trembled. 'Does that make any sense?'

He ran his hands hungrily down her back. 'Oh, Laura, what complications we make for ourselves.'

She knew that he didn't understand and she didn't expect him to. And she felt desperately guilty because of all the times she had pushed him away. But in spite of that, his eyes were devouring her and she knew that she wanted him more than ever.

'You're beautiful, Laura. Each time I see you, I see something else.' He held her against him as they stood in the hall. 'I told you once you had strength. And today you gave me strength. I felt so close to you.'

She felt his chest tighten and she closed her eyes, content just to be in his arms and feel his strong body against her.

Finally he drew away, his voice husky and low as he spoke. 'Maria? Is she still up?'

'She's in her room.'

'May I see her?'

She took his hand and led him to Maria's room. She was sitting in her little play-pen, happily playing with her toys. He walked over and hunkered down, the knotted shoulder muscle under his shirt straining against the restriction of cloth. 'Hello, little one,' he murmured. 'What have you there?'

She beamed him a smile and offered him her toy, a little rainbow-coloured car. He reached in and lifted her into his arms. 'Let's see how fast it goes.' He grinned and sat down on the sofa bed with Maria beside him. He bent forward and rolled it on the floor and Laura sat down and rolled it back. Maria giggled, wriggling her little body off the sofa and down onto the floor. Going on all fours, she followed it, plucking it from Laura's hands with a cry of delight. Then she struggled away and pulled herself up on the sofa again with an expression of triumph.

Laura laughed and Antonio chuckled. He sat forward, his face animated and happy. 'Push your car to me, *bambina*,' he called softly, and Maria studied him, her bright little eyes watchful as she considered his words.

Then something wonderful happened. She took one wobbly step and then another. Laura held her breath. Unaided, she fell into Antonio's open arms.

'Well done!' he cried, swinging her up above his head.

'She's walking,' Laura breathed incredulously. 'But she's only just ten months old.'

'And I am here to witness it.' He chuckled as Maria's cries of delight filled the room.

A shiver went down Laura's spine as she watched, fascinated, for the next ten minutes as her ten-month-old daughter explored every inch of her room on two tiny feet.

They spent a joyous hour with Maria, her new-found skills making them laugh and almost cry. And when she finally slept, it was with her thumb in her mouth, her body curled under the sheet.

Laura switched on the nightlight and bent to kiss Maria's silky head. She smelt of Antonio's lemons and her own sweet baby scent. Antonio waited at the door until she went to him and they stood for a moment, watching Maria.

'I'm glad you were here,' Laura whispered as Antonio's arms snaked round her waist.

'Are you, *caro*?' He turned her slowly to look at him.

She nodded. 'Very.'

'I'm glad, too.'

She reached up and touched his face. 'I'll always remember this day.'

He trickled his hands into her hair and their eyes locked and Laura wondered how this could all feel so right. She wasn't going to question it. All she knew was that tonight was made for them, for the joy and laughter that her little girl had brought and for the deep, pent-up yearning that now clawed in her stomach to be released.

She knew he felt it as well as he bent to kiss her and the passion and yearning was all there, but held in check, his mouth warm and inviting but without demand. His body trembled under her hands as her fingers traced the bunched, athletic muscle that was tensed across his shoulders, revealing tight self-control.

'Laura, I warned you…' he muttered, his dark eyes glittering in the light of the hall. 'Tell me to go now, because beyond this moment…'

She felt her heart race unevenly. 'I don't want you to go.'

'You are certain?'

She was never more certain of anything in her life. She wanted this night for herself, for the release of her need and for other, more complex reasons that she still couldn't put into words.

'I want you, *mi amore*.'

Her bones felt as if they were melting inside her body. For a long moment they stayed there, the passion burning between them, knowing that soon they would be together in a way that had been destined since Maria's birth.

Her precious baby had come into the world in a wonderful way. Despite all the unhappiness of the past, Antonio had delivered Maria, had been responsible for her safe entrance. He had cared for her in illness and witnessed her first small steps on this beautiful earth.

Laura took a deep, shuddering breath. She wasn't going to think of what might happen tomorrow. She was going to take what happiness she could from tonight and make it for ever her own.

*   *   *

Antonio was astonishingly tender as they stood in her bedroom, the door closing them in their own little world. He drew the straps of her dress over her shoulders as gently as if he were peeling a gauzy wrapper from flowers. His fingers were unbearably soft against her skin and she could feel the willing throb of her body in response.

She tried not to let emotion swamp her. But he tugged off his shirt and let it fall to the floor and the exquisite form of his tall, broad-chested body was enough to send a bolt of fresh craving through her.

Even though she'd seen him dripping wet on the day he'd rescued Mitchell Fraser, she hadn't really taken in how magnificent he was. The colour of his skin was a rich, glossy gold and the thick black mat that covered his chest only stopped to curl in the well of his throat. And when her eyes lowered, she saw the twisted whorls snake seductively below the waistband of his trousers.

'Laura?' he said, and she looked up guiltily.

'I…I'm out of practice,' she stammered, but his eloquent eyes didn't blink.

'Then we'll learn together,' he murmured, drawing her fingers to the buckle of his belt to slide out the rich, dark leather from the clip. His hands teased down the bodice of her dress and found the white, simple curve of her bra. His gaze burned fiercely as he released the little clip and her breasts spilled free.

She almost jumped, but he took her chin between his hands and kissed her, his tongue probing softly, reassuringly. Then all his emotion was released as she responded and his mouth curved over hers with such passion that she melted and clung to him.

Somewhere in their embrace her dress fell to the floor, as did his trousers, and he lifted her, taking her in his arms to lay her on the bed. She lay there, wondering if it was possible to want someone so much that she didn't care what she looked like, aware of the insistent, demanding heat pooling between her legs.

He eased himself beside her, covering her body with a blanket of fire, his eyes scorching their way over her body in a way that seemed so frightening and wonderful at the same time.

Frightening because she knew she was ready for him and wonderful because it was so different from before, when she had given herself only to please Mark and their love-making had ended so unsatisfyingly.

Antonio's love-making was so different. So out of this world. He was tender and gentle, but firm and provocative, and each movement of his hand over her body was sensual enough to make her want more.

'Laura, I have told you before you are beautiful,' he whispered, almost grinding his teeth as his warm breath flowed over her breasts. 'But I didn't realize how beautiful.' He kissed their throbbing peaks so shamelessly exposed for his attention and just when she thought she could bear no more and her hands were dragging him towards her, he slid his mouth to her tummy and kissed the flat, tight plane of skin above her white panties.

She could hardly stand the pleasure as his tongue caressed her. Soon dispensing with the flimsy little slip of white, she lay naked, hungry for more.

'Caro…' he muttered as their passion burned, 'have we protection?'

She nodded, and reached out to the side table where she had placed her purchase from the chemist. But nothing could interrupt their desire as a few seconds later he pressed his mouth over her lips.

His hard, strong back arched over her, his eyes filled with flames of ebony fire that seemed to touch her own.

Her own green eyes flooded with a love that she knew she mustn't reveal and she slipped against him as he lifted her, his strong forearm curved under her spine. In her wildest dreams she had never imagined making love could be like this. Rapture flooded her soul as he entered her, demanding her response with expert, exquisitely pleasurable rhythm. Her need swelled, became as powerful and as hungry as his and united them in a moment of triumph that could not have been better timed.

She cried aloud and clung to him. Her face was buried in the hollow of his shoulder as he surged inside her, releasing deep, aching groans of exultation. Eventually he relaxed, lowering himself, one arm protectively across her.

Her heart was still beating crazily, her body shuddering as he left her, filled with a completeness that she had never experienced in her life. She turned to face him, drawing herself close as his arm enclosed her and they lay face to face, their sweat-dampened bodies resting across the tumbled sheets.

'Oh, Laura,' he whispered, his husky voice doing things to her that shouldn't be happening after what she'd just experienced. 'You are sweetness itself, do you know that?'

A thirst that she had thought slaked dried the inside of her mouth. 'I just know how wonderful that was.'

Antonio traced a wisp of hair from her face. 'Would you tell me the truth?'

She smiled with kiss-bruised lips. 'The truth...yes.'

'I was selfish—'

'No. *I* was selfish.'

He gave a grim little smile. 'Then I am happy.' He pulled her against his chest and ran his fingers through her wild tangle of curls, until finally their breathing slowed to an even rhythm. When she knew he was asleep she went to check on Maria, but moments later she was sliding back in to the warm nest of their love-making. Automatically his arms reached out to bring her against his chest.

'Is she asleep?' He kissed her ear and deliciously nibbled her lobe as one hair-roughened thigh trapped her slender body against him.

'Out for the count,' she whispered as his hands ran the length of her naked body and the breath jammed hard in her lungs. His tongue delved into her mouth and her heart hammered madly as they made love again, totally lost in their own little world.

Laura woke the next morning still locked in Antonio's grasp, one hand protectively curved around her breast, the other snaked under her waist. She wriggled out and went to the loo and checked Maria who was still asleep. Then she snuggled back in beside him and his eyes flicked open, their beautiful coal-black centres gazing sleepily into hers.

'Good morning.' He grinned and she smiled, wondering as she looked into his eyes how it was possible to feel so happy. So content.

The sun was breaking through the blinds, spreading a fan of hazy light over the bed. It was quiet, not yet six, and the breeze blew in through the window and gulls called and broke the fragile silence.

'Sleep well?' she murmured, and his smile widened, his sleep-filled eyes drugged and lazy.

'What little there was of it—yes. I slept well.'

'Is that a complaint?'

'No, more of a...hope.' His smile faded and she knew as he pulled her close what he meant. But it was too much to take in, too much to assemble in her thoughts. She hadn't imagined she'd feel like this, so completely and utterly fulfilled. What had she been thinking yesterday, she wondered, when the news of Mitchell Fraser had hit them both so hard and they'd sought comfort from one another?

A one night's panacea to balance the emotional see-saw? A brief rest in another place? Or unadulterated lust that had proved too much to bear and had had to be satisfied, temporarily?

As she looked into his face, she didn't know what her true motives had been. Only that yesterday something inside her had reached out and touched his soul. And he had responded and here they were and it had been the most wonderful experience of her life.

'Don't let's talk about tomorrow,' she whispered, his

hands wrapping her into a cocoon of warmth that she couldn't bear to think of leaving. Not yet. Not until it was time…

'Is Maria awake?' he asked gruffly, his lips a fraction away on the pillow.

'Not yet.'

'What is her usual time?'

Laura snaked one long leg across the powerful leg beneath her. 'Seven, seven-thirty. She'll call out. She always does.'

'Then, there's time…?' He gazed at her and she nodded and soon his kisses were burning her mouth and taking her to heaven again. She put every single stray thought from her mind as he made love to her. His tongue was moist and urgent and his body was on fire as his kisses went on and on. His chest heaved with tension, so that she could feel the crisp, thick mat of chest hair that she longed to expose and explore. Again.

And she did, her fingers wantonly seeking him, slower and more adventurous now, her appetite for him increasing. A little fact of life that she refused to acknowledge for the moment and told herself she would think about later. When he'd gone. And she could put all that had happened into context.

CHAPTER TWELVE

LATER, of course, never came.

Neither did the careful consideration of what she had done. It didn't happen because Laura's mind played the oldest trick in the world. It convinced her she was in love. Not the love that she'd experienced with Mark, but a love that filled every part of her being and opened the floodgates to the possibility of life change.

Could she somehow make her life with this man? Could she trust Antonio not to hurt her or Maria? Could she surrender her plans for the future? So many questions flooded her mind that weekend.

The questions were there, though. Little embryo cobwebs, not fully fashioned, strung in the shadows of her mind. They were too vague to acknowledge, too ephemeral. When he held Maria or played with her, holding her hand as she tottered over new pathways, the questions lit up like little nightlights, burning vividly in her mind.

She put them on hold, though, when they drove back to Canzone and fetched his overnight bag and fresh clothes. And later, when they strolled down to the harbour, pushing the buggy between them. And in Molly's café, when they talked over coffee and fed Maria muffins, then wandered idly back up to Sea Breeze. She kept all the doubts at bay.

It wasn't until the evening they tormented her. As he played with Maria in the garden and stretched out on the seat and laughed and talked baby talk. It wasn't until then they came pouring through like water escaping a drain.

Was there a chance of a future in Charbourne? Could she settle for less and cope financially? What if she failed again? What if she made a terrible mess of it all? What if, to him, this was just a fling? What if he *wanted* her to go? Was that why this was so good—because he didn't have to commit himself?

Saturday night they ate supper in the dining room, lit by candles and a single lamp that reflected the dark, glittering harbour. They made love afterwards, falling asleep in each other's arms at some insanely late hour. And on Sunday they drove to the country and followed wild country lanes. And laughed. And got to know all the little things that lovers needed to know.

And when Maria had walked them to exhaustion and she lay asleep in bed, they collapsed on the sofa in Aunt M.'s tiny lounge and made love there, too. In the dusk, with the long windows thrown open and the stars twinkling in.

It was only on Monday morning that the doubts washed back. Laura woke to an empty bed and her heart pounded as she struggled out and wrapped herself in her robe. Maria was still sleeping so she went to the lounge and found him there, standing in sexy white underpants, naked to the waist, using his electric razor. Relief swamped her and yearning cramped her tummy as her eyes devoured his beautiful body, recalling just about every moment they'd made love.

He turned and flipped off the razor and pulled her into his arms. He smelt intoxicating, his own special brand of male and sleep and love-making.

'You're up early,' she whispered, as he kissed her, the square inch of unshaven beard that was left deliciously grazing her skin.

'I was going to make you coffee,' he murmured with a little growl of delight as she snuggled into him.

'I won't be able to look at you at work,' she teased, as he drew back her wild curls and ran his eyes over her face. 'I'll just have to ignore you.'

He tipped up her chin and searched her eyes. 'You don't want the others to know?'

'Do you?'

He frowned thoughtfully. 'For your sake, *mi amore*, perhaps discretion is best.'

She didn't know if that was technically good or bad. And the machine of her mind threw up a thousand negatives, which inevitably made it bad. But he loosened her belt and ran his hands inside her robe and sighed longingly as it flowed to the floor.

'Come back to bed,' he groaned. 'We've time.'

She wasn't sure if they had but they went and their love-making was urgent and a little desperate. Then Maria woke and they had to scramble up and organize themselves.

Antonio showered and when he was dressed and looking immaculate in white shirt and dark trousers, he walked with Maria in the garden and trailed her patiently round the flower-beds whilst Laura got ready.

After breakfast, they waved him goodbye from the dining-room window. The four-wheel-drive moved off with a toot of the hooter and Laura stopped herself—just—from weeping.

She didn't know why she wanted to weep. Only that she did. Which was ridiculous, because on the surface everything was perfect.

Too perfect, she realised as she gathered her bags and rushed them all into the car and drove Maria to the crèche.

It was a glorious July, full of sunshine, and Charbourne was bustling. Each day the centre got busier and Laura longed for the days when Antonio wasn't on call and they'd meet after work. They'd walk for miles along the beach with Maria or play ball in the garden or eat alfresco at Canzone.

Laura loved the long, sultry evenings and the hot, sweet nights wrapped against him, her arms and legs tangled with his as they slept under cool cotton sheets. She hated the mornings when they said goodbye. And pretended to be different people at work.

One Tuesday morning Laura walked into surgery and

Michelle told her that Bethany was sitting in the little rest room.

'My parents are with Dr Dallori,' Bethany said as Laura walked in and sat beside her. 'I've decided to keep the baby. My boyfriend said he's going to stick by me. We told Mum and Dad and they were really cool about it. I think Mum is relieved it's someone of my own age, not some old guy that I was trying to protect.'

Laura hid her smile. 'So, are you staying at home?'

Bethany grinned. 'My brother says he'll move into the box room if Dad fits his computer with a modem for the internet. Then me and the baby can move into his room, which is a lot bigger.'

Just then Antonio and the Grahams appeared at the door and Louise Graham arched an eyebrow at her daughter. 'You've heard the news, then,' she said sharply. 'Heaven knows how we'll manage but I suppose we will. Just look at you, popping out of your things already.'

'Oh, Mum, stop going on,' Bethany complained irritably, and stood up, running her hands proudly over her bump. She looked at Laura under her lashes. 'See you at clinic tomorrow,' she said, and Laura watched the trio depart, already into another dispute as they walked along the hall.

Antonio met her gaze and rolled his eyes. 'See you later,' he mouthed.

She watched his tall figure disappear, his broad shoulders swinging into his room along the hall.

Laura sighed and sat for a moment, thinking. It wasn't going to be an easy ride for the Grahams. There would probably be a few family battles along the way. But Bethany's baby would be loved and acknowledged and given a place to grow and, really, Bethany couldn't ask for more.

The days passed and the temporary residents and holiday-makers quickly filled any spare spaces that the surgery could offer. When Antonio wasn't on call, they would stroll

down to the harbour with Maria or stay overnight at
Canzone and wake to the view of the bay and the smell of
scented blooms on the vine outside.

Or if the mood took them they'd buy take-aways and eat
them in Aunt M.'s little lounge. But always there were the
long, hot nights spent in each other's arms that she wished
would never end. A few more people looked at Sea Breeze
and July melted to August, and even then Laura didn't let
herself think about September.

Then one Saturday afternoon in August her mobile rang.
She sat in stunned silence as the estate agent told her that
Sea Breeze had been sold.

'Are you serious?' she asked, trying to catch her breath.

He told her that his clients had offered the full price and
they weren't involved in a chain. After the call she sat in
a daze. Sea Breeze had been sold. Her mind flew from one
thing to another and she felt a little sick and giddy. There
was a knock at the door and she ran to it, hoping it was
Antonio and she could pour everything out. But it was
Rachel, Mrs Kent's granddaughter.

'Grandma's made tea. Can you both come?' she asked.

Laura couldn't refuse. She hadn't seen the Kents for
weeks. And she should be on a high—celebrating. So she
said they'd be along.

A lead weight had formed in the pit of her stomach since
the estate agent's call. This was what she had been waiting
for. This was the beginning of her future. But it was the
one she had planned before falling in love with Antonio.

Just as she was about to leave, Antonio arrived. His eyes
were dark and sexy, if a little tired, and they seemed to
engulf her as he reached out and drew her into his arms. 'I
missed you,' he whispered, his breath warm on her neck
as he sniffed her hair. 'You smell gorgeous.'

She laughed lightly—too lightly—clumsily hiding her
emotions. 'We're going to Mrs Kent's for tea. Her granddaughter's there. Come with us.'

'Girls' thing, eh?' He grinned, straightening his back and letting her go. 'Think I'll take a rain-check.'

'Will you be here when we come home?'

'Where else?' His eyes were full of promise. 'I'll be waiting.'

She left, only to count the minutes until she returned.

Mrs Kent had put on a delicious tea. It was one of her grandchildren's birthdays and by the time the festivities were over Laura realized it was almost six.

When they arrived home she found a note on the table, a few words and a trio of kisses beneath. Antonio had been called out and said he'd be back as soon as he could. But it wasn't until well after nine that he returned.

He looked shattered. His shirt was filthy, with oil and grease all over it. 'Oh, lord,' she whispered, her hand flying to her mouth. 'What's happened? Are you hurt?'

'No,' he assured her. 'I'm OK. There was a pile-up on the motorway. An oil tanker went into a barrier. The cars on the other carriage way took the brunt.'

'Oh, lord,' she sighed, 'how grim.'

He nodded, wearily sinking into a chair. 'The hospital was struggling with staff on holiday and a flu bug raging in the wards. The worst timing ever. All available help was called in.'

They talked for hours because she knew he needed to. Then she ran him a bath and afterwards they sat and drank nightcaps, reluctant to sleep.

But exhaustion took him in the end and she lay beside him, listening to his breathing, vowing she would give him her news tomorrow or perhaps the next day. Or whenever the time felt right after this.

Laura went from day to day, telling herself they'd talk when Antonio didn't have so much on his mind. The motorway accident had claimed nine lives and a shadow seemed to have been cast over them for a while. And just when they seemed to be recovering, a virus wreaked havoc and sent the waiting lists sky-high.

She knew she was making excuses. Trying to justify her silence. Or, more honestly, she admitted, she wanted him to talk about September. To ask her what she was going to do after she left the surgery. But he didn't. And the days marched dangerously on to the end of August.

It seemed as though a great wave had engulfed her and was rolling her along, and she was helplessly caught up in it. Work was frantic and each day went faster than the one before.

Whenever Antonio was with Maria he seemed happy and grounded, and when they were in bed their love-making was mindless. But that was what troubled her. It was as if they were making up for words they just couldn't bring themselves to say.

One Friday in early September, Laura took the morning off to see the solicitor completing the necessary papers for the sale of Sea Breeze. Afterwards, she drove straight to the centre, a little weak at the knees. She hadn't expected the paperwork to run so smoothly, but it had and now there were only contracts to sign.

She had to tell Antonio. There was no question now. After this week, she had just seven days left at work. Why hadn't he brought up the subject? It was as if he was ignoring it, as though the end wasn't in sight.

So she parked her car and walked towards the surgery. She'd tell him this afternoon, the instant she saw him. Somehow she'd find the words. Somehow. And tonight they'd talk it all out and find answers to their problems…

She'd just reached the doors when she heard the growl of an engine. She turned and there it was, the four-wheel-drive crawling in across the gravel. Her heart leapt. She couldn't believe how much she'd missed Antonio. Last night he'd been on call and hadn't slept over. She wanted to run to him, hold him in her arms and tell him everything.

And she would. But slowly, calmly, sensibly.

As she was about to move, another car drove in. It parked and a familiar dark-headed young woman climbed out. Antonio walked towards her and they embraced, and Laura's legs buckled. She fought down the dizzy weakness, wrenched her eyes away and fled into surgery.

An old girlfriend? A current one? Did it matter? The mystery woman he kept appearing with was still part of his life. Yet he had never mentioned her. And I've never asked, Laura berated herself a dozen times during the afternoon as she struggled to concentrate. Why hadn't she asked? Because she had blocked everything from her mind these last few months, came the truthful answer. She'd been in her own little world and she'd wanted it that way.

She managed to avoid him all afternoon. It was easy enough because their lists were full. Mrs Frost came in at two-thirty with chronic indigestion and Becky passed her over as usual. Laura gave the woman a gentle lecture on her eating habits, the result of a precarious diet of sweet and fatty foods that she'd maintained on holiday with her daughter-in-law, and then it was almost three.

She fought to keep up with her list and just about managed by the time she was due to leave. Normally, she would have checked whether Antonio was free and, if he was, said goodbye. But she couldn't bring herself to today. So she shut her computer down and drove like the wind to collect Maria. By the time they arrived home, she felt lost and abandoned and utterly wretched.

Would Antonio ring her? They had no firm plans for the weekend. But by the time Maria went to bed he hadn't called and she dragged herself around the place, doing little jobs that didn't really need doing.

Was she admitting she still wanted him if he was seeing someone else? Had she sunk so low that she was prepared to believe her own fantasies? Was this Mark all over again?

Not entirely, replied the voice of reason in her head. Mark had promised her everything. Antonio, nothing. Not a future or commitment of any kind. He'd never suggested she change her mind about leaving Charbourne. Had she just been indulging herself in a fruitless affair that could never mean anything more?

Her eyes filled with self-pitying tears. Was Antonio with the woman tonight? Was he holding her in his arms, loving her the way Laura yearned to be loved? And Maria? Had his affection for her been genuine? Real tears flowed then and she sat in the silence, the house never seeming more empty than it was now.

Antonio tapped on the door at nine and she ran to open it, scrubbing her eyes quickly with her sleeve as she recognized his tall shadow through the glass. She knew what she must look like because he stood where he was when he saw her.

'Laura?' A frown crumpled his forehead. He stepped forward and she closed the door behind him. She'd never given him a key and the irony wasn't lost on her now, for he'd never asked for one. He drew her into his arms and she went eagerly, forgetting for a few blissful moments what had happened that day. The warmth of his body drove through his shirt and sent a torturous thrill through her own. Then she remembered the way he had held that other woman, only hours ago—and she pushed away.

'We'd better talk,' she said, and the composure of her own voice shocked her. Only moments ago she'd been a victim to the steel-cold fear that had haunted her for weeks.

She walked to the little lounge and sat on the sofa. He took the big armchair opposite, leaning forward, elbows on knees. 'Where were you this morning?' he asked before she could speak.

'At my solicitor's. The sale for Sea Breeze has been agreed.'

He stared at her in silent surprise, his dark eyes going

over her face with a blank expression until slowly the meaning of her words took effect. 'Why didn't you say so?'

'You haven't asked,' she replied simply.

'I've been waiting for you to tell me.'

Suddenly she felt calm. It was a relief to have unburdened herself. Even though she sensed what might be coming might be no less painful than the keeping of her secret, she was glad it was out in the open.

'Was that the reason you left today without seeing me?'

'I did see you,' she replied, only this time her voice shook. 'I'd just parked my car and then you drove in, and another car arrived. I saw—' She stopped, the words *I saw you in another woman's arms* too painful to say as hot tears pricked dangerously at her eyes.

He sat very still, gazing at her. His heavy lids lifted, revealing the beautiful dark orbs below.

'What—exactly—did you see?' His voice was hard-edged and cold.

'I saw...I saw the two of you...' she blurted, sniffing back the tears. To her surprise he didn't turn a hair, just kept staring at her as though not recognizing her.

'And?'

What did he want, a full description? she thought, suddenly angry, relieved that anger was helping her to face this. 'I saw you *together*,' she answered, her response as cold as his.

A muscle worked tightly in his jaw. 'So that is what this is all about? Your tears, your distress, your coldness?'

'What did you expect, Antonio?' She would have laughed if she wasn't in so much pain.

'Trust,' he said, his voice rough and uneven.

'Trust?' she repeated, staring at him. 'But I saw what I saw.'

'And put your own interpretation on it.' He surveyed her from under black brows.

'What other interpretation is there?' she croaked, shaken.

'The true one, which you have taken pains to overlook.'

She was stunned. He was taking this so calmly. What other possible explanation could there be? She hadn't seen this woman just once with him, but three times.

She fought back the emotion. 'I saw you—'

'With Gabrielle.' One black eyebrow twitched up. 'You believed me capable of deceiving you.'

A heartbeat lodged in her throat. Who was Gabrielle? The name seemed familiar, but she couldn't place it. His face darkened as he sank back in the chair, his fingers gripping the arms, all his masculinity and strength embodied in the expression that flooded his face.

After what seemed an eternity, he spoke. 'You saw me *greeting* a woman. And, on reflection, if the situation had been reversed...' He paused, his words hanging in the air. 'However, I had hoped over the past months you would have learned to trust me, but...' He stopped, his mouth clamped into a grim line. 'The girl you saw is my cousin Gabrielle. Her father is my uncle and the relative with whom *Mamma* stayed for a while. It was my intention that I would introduce you soon. Gabby is to be married and came to give us an invitation.'

Laura dragged in a breath as Antonio's words became clear. The enormity of her mistake overwhelmed her. She had judged him wrongly. 'I...I'm so sorry,' she breathed, closing her eyes briefly to stop the tears falling. 'I don't know why I jumped to the conclusion—'

'Because you wanted to?' he posed, reaching across to draw the tip of his finger under her wet lashes. 'Laura, your master plan for happiness will not go unchallenged. Not with any man. At some point, you will have to trust again. That is, if you don't wish to live a very lonely life.'

She felt a dreadful sadness inside her. His words struck home, to her soul. She yearned to reach out and draw him to her and tell him her master plan counted for nothing if he wasn't part of it.

But he stood up and walked to the door. 'I think I should give you a little space, *caro*,' he said, trapping his lip under his white teeth as his brow furrowed. 'You have much to think about. No one else can decide the answers for you.'

Laura wanted to tell him that all she wanted was him. That she loved him with all her heart and she had been an idiot in trying to ensure that she and Maria would never be hurt again.

Life didn't provide guarantees of happiness. Antonio was right. But the words clogged painfully in her throat. What if she wasn't able to trust again? What if she could never truly set aside her fears of rejection? Perhaps the truth was that, after Mark, she would never be able to trust enough to love.

So all she could do was to watch him leave as the late summer evening closed in around her.

CHAPTER THIRTEEN

LAURA kept busy over the weekend and phoned Shelley about Sea Breeze. But Shelley was on a high and had a new man in her life. And afterwards Laura wondered if buying somewhere with her friend was still an option. They'd lost touch for a while and Laura felt responsible for that.

She'd been too involved with Antonio to make more than a couple of calls. And Shelley had been busy, too. They'd been caught up in different lives. So different from before…

But Shelley phoned her back on Sunday morning and things seemed fine again, and they talked endlessly about possibilities and the price of properties. Finally Laura said she'd drive back the following weekend with some of her things. She didn't have a lot. Hardly more than she'd come down with a year ago. Then when she was settled at the flat, she'd call back for the rest.

The day straggled on and when the phone was silent and she tried to pretend it was all for the best, the little voice inside her screamed that it wasn't. It felt like the end of the world.

So she walked down to the sea with Maria and played on the sand and paddled in the water. The visitors were few and far between and Molly's café was empty. Laura couldn't go inside. It held too many memories. She plastered on a smile and waved to Molly and pushed the buggy energetically back up the hill.

When Maria was asleep that night, Laura indulged in sweet torture. And sat in the dining room for the last time. She lit a candle and remembered every word, every look

nd kiss, and when the pain was too much she blew it out,
vatching the shadows fade and die.

She didn't sleep. She'd known she wouldn't. She
readed Monday and yet she yearned for it. She longed for
ne sight of Antonio, just a glimpse, some panacea for the
ddiction that was gnawing at her soul.

But when she arrived, he was out on his calls and she
idn't see him all day.

And when Becky asked her to meet everyone for a drink
n Wednesday, she almost chickened out.

'Just the girls,' Becky pleaded. 'A quick one to say good-
ye.'

She could have used Maria as an excuse but she didn't,
nd Mrs Kent was only too pleased to sit with Maria.
Michelle, Joanne, Mo and Maggie turned up, and they
•rought flowers and chocolates. Laura was touched.

But she was home by ten and by Thursday she had
ounted the times she'd seen Antonio on one hand. He'd
hrown her a smile as he'd left at lunchtime and a wave as
hey'd driven by each other in their cars. Once they'd al-
nost passed in the hall—but he'd turned off and she'd hur-
ied away.

Didn't he care? Didn't he want to see her before she
eft? She wrestled with going to see him or driving up to
Canzone del Mare but her pride wouldn't let her. On
Friday, Liam Ray and Jamie Collins bade her farewell, and
inally Antonio and Ravi.

'We'll miss you,' Ravi said and hugged her as they stood
n the hall between patients.

Then someone called and Ravi rushed off and they were
ilone. 'How have you been?' Antonio asked, and she was
parely able look in his face.

'Fine,' she lied. 'And you?'

He gave a little grunt. 'Laura, shouldn't we talk? This
loesn't seem like the way...' He paused, as if wrestling
with himself, 'to say goodbye.'

Goodbye.

Laura swallowed as memories rushed back with that on
word—his touch, his smell, the way his body curled roun
her in bed and made her feel whole again and complet
and then the sense of loss that followed with a sickenin,
certainty.

'We should have, yes,' she replied unsteadily.

'Why didn't we?' He stared at her, his dark eyes search
ing her face.

'I'm not sure. But I—'

'Nurse Bright?' A voice split their little world apart. 'I'n
so glad I caught you, dear. I hear you're leaving,' Mrs Fros
called, almost falling into them as she came to a halt.

'Steady.' Antonio smiled, catching her arm.

'I wish I was, Dr Dallori,' Mrs Frost sighed. 'I'm all a
twos and threes these days.' She turned breathlessly t(
Laura, patting her neatly permed hair. 'I've just brough
you a little something to say thank you.' She pressed
Cellophane-wrapped single rose into Laura's hands. 'I won
dered if I could have one last word with you about m)
indigestion?'

Laura nodded, her eyes meeting Antonio's. 'Yes, ot
course.'

'I do hope I'm not a bother.'

His eyes were still locked with Laura's above the smal
grey head. 'I'd better let you get on.'

'Oh, we'll not be long,' Mrs Frost assured him as she
leant on Laura. 'You can have her back soon, Dr Dallori.'

His eyes trapped Laura's for a few seconds more, then
Mrs Frost moved on and drew Laura with her.

'He's such a nice young man,' Mrs Frost said as Laura
led her into her room and she sank down into a chair. 'He's
not married, is he? A wonderful catch for some lucky
woman.'

Laura didn't respond as she closed the door, her eyes
sweeping in vain over the deserted hallway.

The City felt—and looked—so different. The first-floor flat
that she'd shared with Shelley and had once thought so

comfortable felt cramped and colourless. Even the view from the window was depressing. Her double room afforded a glimpse of the tiny park below, but the high-rise development opposite seemed to overshadow the trees and greenery.

It felt like a foreign country. Their shared flat had been her home throughout her training, but now she found it difficult to grasp that she'd lived here with Shelley. It didn't seem like a year she'd been away, more like a lifetime.

'So, what's the verdict?' Shelley's noisy whisper brought her back to the present and she turned from the window. Maria was asleep on the small divan next to Laura's double bed. Shelley squatted on a beanbag in jeans and bright pink shirt, eager to know what Laura thought of her boyfriend.

'He's great.' Laura nodded. 'I like him.'

'Yes, but is he—you know—Mr Right?'

Laura laughed softly. 'You tell me.' They'd all shared a meal together that evening and Andy had seemed a really nice guy.

Shelley paused, biting her lip. 'The thing is, he's asked me to move in with him.'

'Oh—I see.' Laura tried not to look disappointed. Obviously Shelley was smitten, and why not? They seemed the perfect couple.

'But there's us,' Shelley said quickly. 'We had plans, too, and I don't want to let you down.'

Laura shrugged. 'We haven't even started looking yet. And I'm not in a rush to find somewhere—not now Sea Breeze has been sold. I'll have a little holiday with Maria first, then look for work. I've one or two ideas up my sleeve.'

Shelley grimaced. 'You're just saying that to make me feel better.'

'Would I?' Laura teased, and Shelley rolled her eyes and sighed.

'I hope you're telling me the truth.'

But as she lay in bed that night, listening to Maria's soft breathing beside her, Laura felt loneliness wash over her. The course of her life had changed yet again now that Shelley was moving in with Andy. It was a setback to her plans but nothing, she reminded herself, grasping at straws, that was as painful as the break she'd made from Antonio.

Even as she'd returned to Sea Breeze four days ago and signed contracts, locking the door of the old place for the last time, she'd still hoped he'd call or ring. But he hadn't and she'd come home in a kind of foggy limbo that seemed like some bad dream.

Laura lay, counting the spherical patterns of light on the ceiling and listening to the noise of the traffic in the street below. It was a monotonous grumble in comparison to the smooth echo of the sea. Would she ever get used to living in the City again?

Of course she would.

But for the third night in a row, she cried herself to sleep.

It was half past three when she woke. The illuminous figures on her alarm clock shone brightly in the darkness. Her first thought was of Maria. She slipped out of bed and went over to her daughter's divan, but Maria was fast asleep, snuggled under the covers.

Laura kissed her cheek and climbed back into bed. Then suddenly something hit the window with a thud and Laura froze.

Could it have been a bird? Or was it something more sinister? She strained her ears as her heart thumped loudly in her ears.

Then a crack shattered the silence and Laura jumped out of bed. She slipped on her robe and picked up the nearest object—a heavy-duty torch from the car. She had no idea what she would do with it, but she felt safer having something solid in her hand.

Moving to the window, she drew the curtain. She had a

clear view of the flats and the street below. All was deserted.

Then a figure moved in the shadows. She froze again. Was it a vandal, a burglar, a drunk? But why alert her to his presence?

She watched for what could only have been seconds but seemed like years as the tall figure stepped onto the pavement and hunched his shoulders under his coat. He saw her and raised his hand in greeting.

It looked like Andy.

A few minutes later Laura was making her way out of the front door and down the short flight of stairs that led to the stairwell. A security light was activated as she hurried down to the front door. By the time she had deactivated the alarm and juggled all the locks, she was wondering why she hadn't woken Shelley.

Perhaps she had reacted so quickly out of relief. Or tiredness. But even though Andy was, for some reason, calling at this unearthly hour, it was friend and not foe who waited outside in the chilly night air.

Her fingers paused on the safety chain as she peered through the crack. Outside the tall figure bent closer. In the light that had automatically flicked on, his black hair gleamed and his breath curled up like smoke.

Laura stared, her green eyes losing their sleepiness as his deep voice filtered through. 'Laura, it's me,' he told her urgently.

She couldn't believe her eyes. *'Antonio?'*

'May I come in?'

She stood still, her knees sagging. 'But why…how…?'

'I'll tell you if you open the door.'

She closed it and slid the chain and he stepped inside, with a wave of cold night air and lemony cologne following him. Her heart pounded as she stared up at him. 'It was you throwing things at my window?'

'Pebbles from the park,' he said as she closed the door again. 'I took a chance that was your window.'

'But why?' She felt as though she were in a dream.

'It is unforgivable to disturb you at this hour. But it was the only way, without waking the household. Laura, I must ask you a question.'

She stared at him, tempted to laugh, shivering under her thin robe. He was here in the flesh, his dark eyes filled with some force of emotion that was eating into his soul. 'A question?' she repeated hollowly.

'Yes. Just one. And I shall leave immediately if the answer is what I fear.'

Her pulse raced as she nodded. 'What is it?'

His chest rose under his coat as he drew in a breath. 'You live here...' he gazed up the flight of stairs to the flat '...with whom?'

Never in a million years would she have guessed he would ask her that. She had told him about Shelley—so why was he asking? It didn't make sense. 'Antonio, you know who I share the flat with...'

'*Mi amore*, tell me again. Please.'

She sighed softly, her green eyes confused. 'It's Shelley, my friend, and, of course, Maria. But why—?'

'This is true?' he demanded, his voice rising.

'Of course it's true.' She laughed. 'Who did you think I shared it with?'

The deep lines of concern that furrowed his forehead disappeared as he closed his eyes, then flicked them open. 'Mark,' he murmured hoarsely. 'I believed it might be Mark.'

Laura stared at him, her brain slowly taking in the meaning of what he had just said. 'Oh, Antonio, you couldn't think that—could you?'

'Your determination to return here was so strong,' he protested as he reached for her hands and pulled her towards him. 'I thought the reason must be Maria's father. I threw pebbles at the window, hoping that it would be you and not Mark who appeared. If it was him, then I would have disappeared into the night.'

Her lips twisted into a soft smile. 'Wouldn't it have been easier to phone?'

'What would I have said?' Smouldering brown eyes bore down on her. 'I hoped you would change your mind. It was the sign I was waiting for. That you would stay in Charbourne.'

'But you said nothing to me.'

'How could I? Your heart's desire was here—or so I thought. You seemed so certain of your path.'

She sighed shakily. 'Never more uncertain.'

'My darling, if only I'd known that.' He kissed her softly, his lips moving uncertainly as he whispered, 'Canzone is full of memories. Of you and Maria—and the days we spent together. They seem *all* of my life, not part of it. I can't recall the time before you. And without you, I have no future.'

'Oh, Antonio,' she breathed as tears of happiness filled her eyes. 'There is only one man in my life. He brought my precious little girl into the world. I grew to love him beyond words.'

'Then I am insanely jealous of this man.' He smothered her laughter with passionate kisses and opened his coat and drew her against his chest, wrapping the warm, heavy cloth over her slender body, his arms locking like a fortress behind her. 'Oh, my sweet Laura, I love you so much.'

An endless breathless silence filled the air as she gazed into his eyes. Was all this true? Had she really heard what he'd just said?

'Come to Canzone. Now.'

'*Now*—this moment?' she asked incredulously.

'Now—this moment.' He nodded.

Tears filled her eyes as his gaze burnt with flames of desire. 'But my clothes and Maria's…'

'Leave them. We'll go shopping together. Buy a whole new wardrobe.'

'You're crazy!' Laughter bubbled in her throat.

'On the contrary. I have changed from a crazy man into a sane one. This is not your world or mine, *caro*. Let's go home to where we belong.'

And finally she understood. This man did truly love her. And by a small step of faith they could move on, one day at a time perhaps but together, as she had always dreamed true love would be.

EPILOGUE

LAURA'S smile was radiant as the photographer captured the moment that would burn brightly in her memory for ever. Signore and Signora Antonio Dallori standing at the entrance of the fourteenth-century church of St Francesco. Above them, a heavy white-bowed ribbon draped across the door to denote a couple in the process of tying the knot. And Maria standing between them, her dark eyes alight with excitement, looking like a tiny princess in her pale lavender Alice in Wonderland gown.

In the soft, clear air the strains of mandolin and guitar mingled with the cries of the diomedei gulls as they soared high above, flying their mystical paths eastward to Mount Tibero and westward to Mount Solaro.

Her arm rested lightly through her husband's, his wedding gift, a bracelet of exquisite mother-of-pearl, draped delicately around her scented wrist, catching the lacy rays of spring sunshine that veiled the joyous gathering.

And her wonderful mother-in-law's wry words still fresh in her mind. *'La buona moglie fa il buon marito.'* A wedding-day proverb spoken by Italian women and passed from generation to generation.

Antonio's mother had murmured it earlier that morning as she had assisted Laura with her silk gown and pearl headdress. Staying at the sumptuous Dallori hilltop villa, the original Canzone del Mare, Laura and Maria had been lavished with care and attention.

Not that Laura had managed to translate the proverb immediately. The hustle and bustle of preparation had been too intense. But given another six months she would, no doubt, be reeling off the language she had grown to love.

It had been Marco, Antonio's brother, waiting for her in
the sleek white limousine outside, who had translated *en
route* to the church.

'A good wife makes a good husband.' Marco had chuckled charmingly, his deep voice so much like Antonio's and
reminding Laura yet again of the potent attraction of all the
Dallori men and the big Italian family into which she was
marrying.

Her mind returned to the present as Antonio moved beside her, stroking aside her ivory veil with tender fingers.
'My beautiful wife, I love you with all my heart.'

She gazed up at him with green fire in her love-filled
eyes. She was in heaven, she decided, unable to remove
her gaze from his full, sensual lips and the dark, potent
gaze lowered upon her.

'And I love you, too, Antonio.'

Looking incredibly handsome in his black tuxedo, silk
tie and white wing collar shirt, he couldn't begin to know
how much she did love him. Maybe one day, when she had
mastered his language sufficiently, she would be able to
describe the joy she was experiencing now.

He bent to draw Maria into a hug and she clasped her
arms around his neck, giggling and squirming as they
laughed together. Laura linked her fingers around her
daughter's shoulder and Maria and Antonio looked up, their
eyes only for her. Laura kissed the tiny forehead and Maria
danced off to join her grandmother who stood close by.

The photographer signalled and Antonio slid his arm
around Laura's waist as they posed one last time at the
church door. His gaze swept hungrily over his bride as it
had done the moment he'd joined her at the altar and they
had made their vows in both English and Italian. Her swift
aptitude to learn and understand his native language had
captivated him. And they had decided that they would honour each other in this way at the moment of betrothal, adding their own personal touch to the religious ceremony.

Suddenly flash bulbs began to go off and everyone was

throwing rice and confetti, the women casting showers of rainbow-coloured stars from their tulle bags, later to be placed alongside the special *bomboniera* basket at the reception.

Beyond the wide-brimmed hats and happy faces, Laura caught sight of the uninterrupted aqua blue of the Gulf of Naples. Her heart almost burst with joy. The sun-caressed waters had her gulping with fresh surprise as the shimmering span of ocean looked second only in texture to her elegant wedding gown.

It was through Elena Dallori's creativity and her Italian seamstress's uncanny ability that Laura was now dressed in the magnificent slim skirt and pearl-encrusted bodice which had caused everyone to gasp as she'd entered the church on Marco's arm. The satin purse that her bridesmaid Gabrielle had given her was linked by a minute silk cord to her tiny waist. Used for the ancient custom of collecting gifts from the guests, even this small detail had been recorded.

Their spring wedding had come as no surprise to anyone but, only six months after the sale of Sea Breeze, it had left Laura feeling breathless and concerned that she wouldn't be prepared. But now it was worth every effort that she had made to travel back and forth to Capri for fittings. The wonderful family get-togethers had enabled her and Maria to adjust to the many new faces. And, of course, to enjoy every moment with her fiancé.

Suddenly, Antonio was propelling her onward, his arm at her back, guiding her protectively through the corridor of tall male figures. Marco, Luca, Pietro and Roberto had formed a guard of honour and looked stunningly handsome in their immaculate tuxedos. Then came their wives and children. Elena Dallori followed, holding Maria's hand as the little girl was surrounded by her cousins, aunts and uncles. But Maria was far too busy to notice Laura as she played with Marco's eight-year-old son, Frederico.

More confetti rained down, covering Laura's ivory veil and everyone shouted, *'Evviva gli sposi! Evviva gli sposi!*

'They are cheering the newly-weds.' Antonio grinned as they ducked the confetti. His lips were close to her cheek and his breath tantalized her skin like quicksilver. Laura blushed lightly as she waved to everyone, aware of the heat of Antonio's eyes as they feasted on his new bride.

Shelley and Gabrielle, her two bridesmaids, were beside them, helping with the long train edged so delicately in spun silk. Dressed in their ivory gowns, embroidered with rich Italian lavender lace, they were radiantly beautiful. Laura hugged them and was swept into the crowd, just managing to cast her bouquet of baby white roses into the air.

A squeal went up as Marco caught them and laughter and cheers went up from his family. His handsome dark eyes met Laura's in a teasing glimmer. *'Grazie*, Laura, *grazie!*' he called with a charming grin, crooking up a black eyebrow at the beautiful flowers, suggesting he wasn't at all displeased.

Then another chant erupted and the guests began clapping, shouting at the top of their voices.

'Bacio! Bacio!'

Antonio pulled her into his arms, his gaze burning fiercely. 'You know what they want, *mi amore*?'

She nodded. It was one word she had learned very early in their relationship. 'I know.'

'Then let's satisfy them…'

Laura looked up into his handsome dark face, her heart so full of love she could barely speak. His head came down and his mouth covered hers with a kiss that left her knees buckling and her slim body, under the silk, leaning against him for support.

The cheer was deafening as they kissed. Antonio's lips were firm and passionate and he supported her against his strong body, fuelling a desire so powerful between them that it seemed to reach her soul. She had never believed that this man would be so much a part of her.

'Our vows are for ever,' he reminded her as he raised his head, his growl just audible above the riot of voices. 'I promise to reward your trust, *mi amore*. I shall make you and Maria happy. More happy than you ever thought possible.'

He didn't need to assure her, but it was wonderful to hear. She knew all her needs, desires and goals would be met in abundance and that they would always be together.

Then suddenly the photographer was beside them, signalling a new direction toward the lush walled garden behind the church. Laura lifted her gown to walk over the path. She gripped Antonio's strong arm and he looked down on her with adoring eyes.

'Just a little while before we are alone,' he promised, and Laura smiled, knowing that she, too, couldn't wait for the moment when they left for their secret destination, a lodge on a tropical island that was to be entirely theirs for two whole weeks.

Safe in the knowledge that Maria would be spoiled and doted on by her grandmother, Laura's heart fluttered at the thought of being entirely alone with her husband.

Her husband!

Freshly translated in her mind, the most cherished words in the world slipped softly from her tongue as they went to the garden.

'*Mio marito…*'

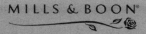

Medical Romance™

TO THE DOCTOR A DAUGHTER *by Marion Lennox*

Dr Nate Ethan has all he needs – a job he loves as a
country doctor and a bachelor lifestyle. Dr Gemma
Campbell is about to change all that! Her sister has
left her with two children – and one of them is Nate's.
She must give Nate his baby and walk away – but
Nate finds he will do anything to stop her leaving…

A MOTHER'S SPECIAL CARE *by Jessica Matthews*

Dr Mac Grant is struggling as a single dad with a
demanding career. Juggling is proving difficult, and he
is aware of his son's longing for a mother. Lori Ames
is a nurse on Mac's ward – a single mother with a
beautiful daughter of her own. Can she bestow upon
them the special care that both children so
desperately need?

RESCUING DR MᴀcALLISTER *by Sarah Morgan*

A&E nurse Ellie Harrison is intrigued by the ruggedly
handsome new doctor at Ambleside. But Dr Ben
MacAllister is playing it cool. The pace and
excitement of the A&E department thrusts them
together and reveals that Ben's growing attraction is
as strong as hers – then Ellie realises he has a
secret…

On sale 2nd May 2003

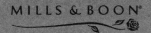

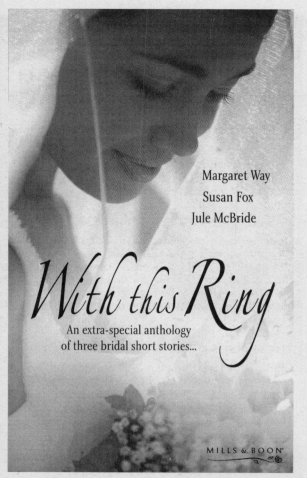

Margaret Way

Susan Fox

Jule McBride

With this Ring

An extra-special anthology
of three bridal short stories...

MILLS & BOON

Available from 18th April 2003

*Available at most branches of WH Smith,
Tesco, Martins, Borders, Eason, Sainsbury's
and all good paperback bookshops.*

0503/024/MB69

2 FREE

books and a surprise gift!

We would like to take this opportunity to thank you for reading this Mills & Boon® book by offering you the chance to take TWO more specially selected titles from the Medical Romance™ series absolutely FREE! We're also making this offer to introduce you to the benefits of the Reader Service™—

- ★ FREE home delivery
- ★ FREE gifts and competitions
- ★ FREE monthly Newsletter
- ★ Exclusive Reader Service discount
- ★ Books available before they're in the shops

Accepting these FREE books and gift places you under no obligation to buy, you may cancel at any time, even after receiving your free shipment. Simply complete your details below and return the entire page to the address below. *You don't even need a stamp!*

YES! Please send me 2 free Medical Romance books and a surprise gift. I understand that unless you hear from me, I will receive 4 superb new titles every month for just £2.60 each, postage and packing free. I am under no obligation to purchase any books and may cancel my subscription at any time. The free books and gift will be mine to keep in any case.

M3ZEA

Ms/Mrs/Miss/Mr ....Initials....................................
                                                    BLOCK CAPITALS PLEASE
Surname ....
Address ....
....
....Postcode................................

Send this whole page to:
UK: FREEPOST CN81, Croydon, CR9 3WZ
EIRE: PO Box 4546, Kilcock, County Kildare (stamp required)